I0785702

Simon Lazarus was born and raised in Cleveland, Ohio where he paved roads and worked on construction with his friend, Bill Pulski. Bill Pulski's wife was headed to the Olympics. This would prove to be very unfortunate.

Officer Olan Oliveria was focused on providing security for the Olympics and intercepting jewel thieves. It might have been quite successful if it hadn't been for the bats.

Ivana Carvalho, the youngest Minister of Health in the history of Brazil, was counting down the days until the tourists of the Olympic Games returned home and she could focus on the emerging bat problem. As it turns out, this was a rather reckless misjudgment.

General Hunter Wallace Wertheim the Third had two objectives - protect the visiting President of the United States at the Olympic Games and control the outbreak of a mysterious bat-borne illness. He would do neither, despite being quite capable and not at all spineless.

Narrated by the Writer, we follow the story of seemingly innocuous people and the events that lead to the end of the world. The apocalypse has never felt so real as we enter the world of bats, sickness, and the last man in Cleveland…

The Last Man in Cleveland

by Danny O'Dea

Curious Corvid Publishing, LLC

Ohio

Copyright © 2021 Danny O'Dea
"The Last Man In Cleveland
Published by Curious Corvid Publishing

All rights reserved.

Printed in the United States of America.

Cover Design by Mark Alexander McClish

https://markmakesart247.wixsite.com/markmakesart247

No part of this book may be used, stored in a system retrieval system, or transmitted, in any form or in any means—by electronic, mechanical, photocopying, recording, or reproduced in any matter whatsoever—
without the written permission from the author, except in the case of brief quotations embodied in the critical articles and reviews.
This is a work of fiction. Names, characters, businesses, places, events, locales, and incidents are either the products of the author's imagination or used in a fictitious manner. Any resemblance to actual persons, living or dead, or actual events is purely coincidental.

Cataloging-in-Publication Data is on file with the Library of Congress.
ISBN hardback: 979-8-9855940-3-4
ISBN paperback: 979-8-9855940-4-1
ISBN (ebook): 979-8-9855940-5-8

www.curiouscorvidpublishing.com

Disclaimer:

It is, first and foremost of all, an author's duty to objectively and honestly relay the facts of their story to their readers, exactly as they occurred. In that spirit, I swear to you now that all the subsequent events of this story, as they are laid out here in the world I created in the bar on the corner of Richmond and Rotaerc, are reported on as precisely as I could recall them.

Chapter 1:
Asphalt

When human beings still roamed the planet Earth, they placed long stretches of rock called *asphalt* along the ground to connect one building to another and rode around in little rooms, so they could roam a little faster. They called the rock *roads* and the roads crisscrossed their way across the face of the planet, like a magnificent asphalt spider web, connecting each human being to every other one with infinite lines of rock.

On these roads, they decided that, in order to ensure their own collective safety, their little rooms could only be permitted to go so fast. They agreed, patted each other on the back, and put up signs advertising how safe their new roads were. These signs were hardly ever given much attention, however, because of how fast the human beings all seemed to drive.

Chapter 2:
The Trouble With Beginnings

"Ugh, you have to change the beginning."

"You don't like it?"

"You do?"

"You hate it!"

"I don't HATE it, exactly, but it starts way too slowly! There's nothing for the reader to grasp on to."

"It's gradual! It's a progression towards the main plot, world building, introduction, all the things necessary for the beginning of a-"

"But it's so *boring*!"

"I think that it needs to be there! Everything in the first chapter comes back later, it sets up the entire rest of the novel."

"If that is how you begin it, how can you expect any of us to want to get to later on?"

"I actually kind of like the way it starts."

"Why?"

"It brings you into the world, you know? It sets the tone and the theme up for the rest of the story."

"Yeah, I see what you mean. Why does the author speak like he does, as if he's a space alien?"

"I guess you'll just have to keep reading to find out, won't you?"

"Hmm, you've got me there. Will you at least think about revising it? Making it more. . . exciting. I love it when you start right with action."

"I'll think about it."

"Will you?"

"For you? Of course."

"It's not *all* that bad, I promise. I just can't wait to know what comes next."

Chapter 3:
Let's Try This Again

Simon Lazarus was born in Cleveland, Ohio, where he lived with many other human beings shortly before the end of man on Earth. This would prove, overall, to be a very bad call on his part.

Cleveland, Ohio, was located inside the country of the United States of America, which was often just called America for short. Simon, as a Black man, had a very tough time in Cleveland, Ohio, due to the fact that it had been decided many years ago that color was a very important thing to pay attention to. Unfortunately for Simon, when they decided this, sometime roughly around the beginning of human beings from elsewhere coming to America, it came to be that the lighter the color you were, the more you ought to matter.

Simon's mother had died when he was just a boy, and he grew up in an apartment with his grandmother. They were often stopped in public.

"Ma'am, is this man bothering you?" more than one police officer had asked Simon's grandmother.

Simon's grandmother was not Black like Simon was, although neither of them were especially tall.

He was built stocky, wide and strong, with the body of a man who had once been a fine athlete, and even through years of neglect the strength had remained. He repaired the roads around the city of Cleveland. The issue of race remained a significant one for many years in America, even after a man named Abraham Lincoln had the courage and imagination to say that it had become embarrassing to own people based on the color of their skin. He was shot in the head for his trouble.

One hundred years after Abraham Lincoln lived and walked around America, a Black man named Martin Luther King Jr. after a German priest (who had himself caused some trouble in the 1500s by inciting a great ruckus when he nailed a piece of paper offering polite criticism of the established religion of the land to a door) pointed out that things had largely not improved all that much.

He was shot for his trouble as well.

Although all of this took place before the time of Simon Lazarus, it still conspired against him to make him incredibly poor, which was the worst thing you could be in Cleveland, Ohio. Being poor was a grave insult to the spirit of the United States of America. If that wasn't enough, Simon was also about to do the worst thing you could possibly do as a poor person in Cleveland, Ohio.

He was about to become very, very, ill.

Chapter 4:
Better?

"Hmm..."

"What do you think? Any better?"

"It's not bad. We'll keep working on it."

Chapter 5:
Incidentally

My wife had once been very ill, too, but in a different way than Simon Lazarus. That was, of course, before she was very dead. She is no longer ill though, so I suppose that some good has come out of the whole ordeal.

Chapter 6:
Tadarida Brasiliensis

Through no fault of my own, I had been born a White male in the Catholic religion. The Catholic religion was considered by as many as two billion human beings to be the most accurate way to thank The Creator for doing all that creating. It had achieved this particular position of moral authority through several centuries of political maneuvering and land grabs in the name of a very nice man who probably lived, named "Jesus Christ."

Jesus Christ is best known for having the courage and imagination to suggest that people stop being so terrible to each other. They nailed him to a tree for speaking so outrageously, but not long afterwards, people began to think that maybe he was on to something. In fact, his followers were so moved by his message that they spent the next fifteen-hundred years proudly murdering other human beings so that they might be moved to spread of the Truth Christ as well.

This strategy proved to be remarkably effective.

Many millions of people who were also born Catholic lived in the country of Brazil, which was located in South America. During my time and the time of Simon Lazarus, who was fictional, and my wife, who was not, this country was going to be the proud host of the Olympic Games. The Olympic Games were a week every fourth year where all the countries in the world stopped fighting wars against each other over land, resources, or religion for a while so that they could watch their favorite athletes swim the breaststroke.

After this week was over and the celebration in favor of universal brotherhood was had, the ceremonial handshakes were exchanged, and the breaststrokers were made to feel very special indeed. It seemed to come, however, that when all this was over, all the countries promptly started fighting each other again, lamenting the atrocities of the world, and awaiting some time four years from then to celebrate brotherhood and breaststroke again.

Human beings were flooding into Brazil by the thousands to watch these games in person and on little television screens and the world was excited, more so than it had been in a long time. Brazil was preparing itself for the influx of tourists; the innkeepers were hiring extra help for the rooms, the police were hiring extra policemen for the robbers, and the robbers were hiring extra policemen for the robbers.

The policemen, although they were under a significant amount of stress on account of having so many people to answer to, were doing quite well for themselves.

Officer Olan Oliveira, for example, was quite pleased with the state of affairs.

"Officer Olan, my family is in town for just the week and my wife's necklace has gone missing."

"Describe it for me."

Officer Olan looked over the man as he described a gorgeous diamond necklace with a sapphire centerpiece. He tried to keep a straight face as the rich American spoke, but already he knew in his gut where he could find such a possession as this. He was going to have to visit the Moroccan.

"Where are you staying sir?"

"At the Grand Hotel."

"And you were keeping the necklace in their vault?"

"Well, no, their prices seemed exorbitant."

Olan smiled. "How about now, sir?"

"Excuse me?"

"The Rio Police Department is incredibly busy at the moment, sir, dealing with the upcoming Olympic Games, so unless you have a reason for me to spend valuable time and man power, I'm afraid there's not much I can do. People lose their jewelry all the time in this city."

The American stood with an expression of baffled indignation, slowly opening and closing his mouth. Olan Oliveira thought the man's expression looked remarkably like a guppy just pulled from water. This thought caused him to smile widely behind his pencil-thin mustache.

"Fine," the American said after a few moments.

He pulled out his wallet and fumbled to remove several bills.

"Fine. Hopefully this will be enough to convince you to do your job."

"We are always looking for ways to help our guests from abroad."

The American turned away muttering, "These people, I swear, without America--"

"Pardon me? You know, I can't believe it slipped my mind, but the police fund is currently accepting donations to help build a daycare," remarked Officer Olan.

Officer Olan Oliveira clipped the bills and placed them in the pocket of his suit. He did hope that he could find that necklace before those Americans returned home, but as he told them, things went missing all the time in Rio.

In addition to millions of Catholics, Brazil was also notably home to millions of *Tadarida brasiliensis,* or the Brazilian squat-tailed bat. Now, I have never seen one of the squat-tails in person, but I have heard them described enough by now to know how to spot one. With their yellow eyes and blunt-tipped tails, they were a remarkably distinctive species of bat and one of the proud indigenous species of the Amazonian rainforest.

As it so happened, they were also dying off at alarming rates and for reasons that local scientists could not determine. A disease, for certain, but where it came from and how it was being spread were seemingly impossible to figure out. Officials from the Brazilian government had more important things to deal with than a slowly dying bat breed; after all, a species went extinct in Brazil once every eleven days and it had been over a week since they released a press statement mourning the apparent loss of the flat headed tree toad. So, when the scientists came to the government with concerns about the health of visitors to the country with this mysterious disease affecting so many local bats, the men and women of the Olympic Planning Committee practically laughed them out of the room. They had much more important matters to deal with.

And so fell another domino.

Chapter 7:
Greeks, Games, and Gods

The Olympic Games, as it happened, were started by the ancient Greeks, a civilization revered for millennia for their immense intelligence and expansive contributions to human knowledge. The Games were named for the perfectly climbable mountain upon which the ancient Greeks believed their gods spent all of their time. The Greeks called this mountain "Olympus." To the best of my knowledge, none of them ever thought to climb up the mountain to check and see if their gods were home.

The gods of ancient Greece were a pantheon of interesting characters, like Zeus, the god of thunder, or Aphrodite, the goddess of love. The ancient Greeks told tall tales of their gods while sitting around the fire late at night. These stories became so famous that they were still being told at the time of Simon Lazarus.

It just so happens that, when I was a young man, I visited the mountain Olympus and climbed it to see the land of the gods for myself. I did not meet anyone named Zeus, but I did meet a striking young woman named Aphrodite.

She had long golden hair pulled into a braid that spilled over her shoulder in loose rivulets down to her waist, and when she approached me she spoke kindness to me in a language older than memory that I did not understand. She giggled at the confusion on my face.

"Come." She spoke to me through a thick accent.

"Excuse me?"

"Me. Come also me."

She grabbed my hand and I followed her down the mountain into an old stone building that seemed to be hewn from the rocks it was built upon.

Although I do not believe she was the goddess, she did charge by the hour, which is not dissimilar from many religious institutions of my day.

Chapter 8:
On the Nature of Mosquitoes

In Cleveland, Ohio, Simon Lazarus was feeling light-headed. This was not due to the bacteria that was deposited in his bloodstream by a stray mosquito and was now rapidly spreading through his small intestine, attacking cells left and right, infecting his very being from his brain to his lungs, already swarming throughout his body and now completely unstoppable.

It was not because of them at all.

In fact, Simon Lazarus was simply dehydrated.

He wiped sweat from his forehead. It was a hot day in a hot summer in Cleveland, Ohio.

"Pulski, you mind if I grab a sip? I sure am parched."

Bill Pulski was a White man who worked in the same construction crew as Simon Lazarus. Over the past twelve years that they had worked together, they managed to overcome the immense hurdle of their respective complexions to become good friends.

Bill Pulski had never really liked being called by his last name. It reminded him of his father, Charles Pulski, who used to beat him after the poor man's wife passed away when Bill was still just a young boy. *Passed away* is a nice term human beings used which here means "dying."

Only once did Bill Pulski protest this nickname. His friends had laughed at him and said, "But Pulski, you love being called that, it's what we've always called you! It is your name, isn't it?"

Pulski laughed along with them and agreed. He had even said that they were right; something must have just been off with him that day.

It was uncomfortable for everyone when grown men divulged their feelings, so the world had silently agreed that instead of feelings, men got to have beer. It seemed like a fair trade at the time.

Simon Lazarus, on the other hand, was remarkably lucky. His father had never once beat him. In fact, his father had never raised a hand toward, or even said a mean word, about him. His father had left the United States of America months before Simon was even born.

"Hey, Pulski! I'm dying here man, could I please get a drink?"

"Huh? Oh, sorry, Simon."

Pulski lowered the canteen from his lips and passed it to his good friend, who in turn took a sip and thanked him. I watched this whole exchange in my head from the bar as I wrote it while the sun beat down on them in Cleveland, Ohio. They were laying down asphalt; building a road.

Simon Lazarus let out a cough that sounded like a dog bark. Pulski looked at him for a second, but then chose to ignore it. He took his canteen back with a nod and drew a sip from it. We all make fatal mistakes, I suppose.

"Thanks, Pulski."

"Don't mention it," Pulski replied. "Goddamn, it sure is hot out here, huh?"

"As hell."

Many of their conversations, similar to many of most humans' conversations, revolved around blatant observations of their surroundings. Human beings felt the innate desire to talk to one another at all times. This was because they were terrified of silence. Silence reminded them of death, a subject all humans were horrifyingly enamored by.

"How's Sarah doing, Bill?"

"Ah, she's fine, I suppose. Gets back from her girls' trip on Monday."

"Oh? Where'd she go?"

"She went to Rio with her friend, Natalie, to watch the Opening Ceremonies. Now that you mention it, I've actually been meaning to talk to you about something. She's been saying she's pretty unhappy with the way things have been recently, you know?"

"How do you mean?"

"I don't know, I don't really get her sometimes. We've spent nine years together, the last two of 'em hitched, I even let her keep that damn tabby cat of hers, and I still don't really get her. You know she cheated on me, back right after we left high school, don't you?"

"You might have mentioned it once or twice."

Bill Pulski had mentioned it to his friend, Simon Lazarus, at least once a month since the incident had occurred.

"I don't know, I was just--"

It was at this moment that Simon Lazarus was called over by small radio called a *walkie-talkie* by a man I decided to name Peyton Brooks.

Peyton Brooks was the foreman of this particular construction site in Cleveland, Ohio, where Simon Lazarus and his White friend Bill Pulski were making a road. This meant he got to wear a special yellow vest that gave him the power to tell the other workers when they could leave. Vests were crucially important to the community of road workers. Without vests, no one would know who was or was not in charge of any given construction crew, and the entire production would devolve into chaos. It was the good fortune, then, for the whole of society, that the vest system was in place and turned out to be as remarkably successful as it was.

"Simon, good to see ya. Sure is hot out here today, isn't it?"

"As hell."

Peyton grunted his agreement.

"So listen, Lazarus, I needja to go an' check on a job out of town some ways. Got a call an' another goddamn road is collapsing in on isself. All the rain this month has got some water poolin' out there, it's happenin' all over the damn county, and it's a pain in my ass, I'll tell you what."

Peyton wasn't born in Cleveland like Simon was.

"You can borruh the work truck s'long as yer back here by six. We just need you to go an' check it all out. I'd deal with 'er myself, but to tell ya the truth the goddamn city still confuses the shit outta me, an' this job here is takin' longer than it should."

So Simon borruhed the truck and left the city to examine the collapsing concrete. He listened to the radio on his way over.

"With the Olympic Games only eight days away," DJ Jeff Sweatman said, "the US of A is rarin' to go! Hoping to beat their historic medal count from four years ago, the United States National Swim Team, in particular Andrew Cordes and Kevin Adrian, the top two breaststrokers for the US squad, aim for gold against their Australian counterparts."

There had indeed been heavy rains for several days, and it showed in the surrounding countryside. Pools of standing water buzzed with mosquitoes all around the small, collapsed bridge that had once spanned a nearby creek. Simon slapped them away by the dozen as they bit at his neck, but some managed to get close enough to bite before buzzing off again.

Simon bent down near the base of the bridge. The ground had eroded beneath it, and there was no structural support in place for a time of such heavy rains like this. Chunks of the bridge had already been washed away. He poked at the asphalt, and it crumbled immediately upon being touched. Sighing and standing again, Simon surveyed the land around the bridge, the narrow two-lane road that went to and from it, and the nearby powerline that had been knocked down recently as well. He reached into his pocket and pulled out a stick of gum. A bridge in this condition would mean days of work, no easy fix would get around that.

Simon shielded his eyes and swore at himself for forgetting a hat. Though he had been outside the truck for no more than a few minutes, Simon had already sweat through his shirt.

It sure was hot out there.

Hot as hell.

Chapter 9:
Businessmen and Gumballs

One of the most important men in my life was named Owen Afton. The influence he had over my entire existence was so immense, I could argue that, without him, the trajectory of my life would have been completely altered by such a degree it would be utterly unrecognizable.

He was also long dead before I ever got the chance to meet and thank him for his influence.

My father moved our family from Centralia, Pennsylvania all the way down to Johnson City, Tennessee, when I was ten years old. I did not want to move, but he was in the road building business and had been offered a lucrative position with Appalachian Asphalt Industries. He wanted to become a Successful Businessman and was well on his way to achieving that dream when he was hired to be the Assistant to the Chief Financial Officer. The man he had been hired to assist was none other than Owen Afton, and he had been the sitting Chief Financial Officer of the corporation for just a little less than twenty-one years.

Two weeks prior to my father officially taking the position, Owen Afton was enjoying time on his farm. He was riding his tractor at dusk along his many rolling, furrowed hills, marveling at yet another scarlet Tennessee sunset over his sprawling estate. His father had been a farmer, and so had his father's father, and so on and so on, presumably all the way back. They had all lived and died on their farms, proud of the land they worked.

Owen Afton was the last in a long line of hard-working, Southern gentlemen. He thought of his life and how far he had come from the world his father had lived in, how he had started with nothing but their small farm, and now was one of the most respected men in the whole of the Tennessee Valley, and how very proud of him his father and grampappy would be if they could see the life he had made for himself and his family. It was while he was contemplating his life and its mysteries and staring off at the fading, red sun that his tractor slid down a patch of grass, rolled over several times down one of his manicured hills, and killed him under its weight. He was dead for fourteen hours, on the same farm that his father had himself passed away on, before anyone found poor old Owen Afton.

Life is funny that way, with fathers and sons.

Appalachian Asphalt Industries had to ensure the transfer of power was as swift and seamless as possible, and so, they hastily rewrote my father's contract and hired him for the newly vacant position of Chief Financial Officer.

This is how my father became a Successful Businessman.

When we moved into our new home in Johnson City, Tennessee, not long after, we hosted a party for all the other successful businessmen in the area. I did not know a single person there, but I did know how to make new friends, and in my pocket, I carried my secret weapon: a small bag of gumballs.

There are few truths I have found to be universal in this world, and this is perhaps the first one I learned that still has never failed to hold: when you find yourself in a situation where there are dozens of people around you but not a soul that you know, the quickest way to make a friend in this crowd is to pick one at random, approach them confidently, and offer them some gum.

So I walked up to the first boy I saw that looked to be my age, introduced myself, and extended a hand.

"Good to meet you." I said, "Would you like a gumball?"

He introduced himself and shook my hand.

"Bill Pulski," my new friend said. "Do you have any red ones?"

From my bag, I pulled out a red gumball and handed it to him.

We ran off and climbed an old bitternut hickory tree that stood in the far front corner of my parents' yard and from its branches we talked about whatever it is that ten-year-olds could possibly think to talk about. A summer storm of deep purple clouds was rolling toward us from a distance.

A young girl approached the tree.

"You two should get out of the tree before the lightning starts."

The air was growing colder, and her hair was fluttering. Bill made a face at her, and she ran off.

"Who was that?" I remember asking Bill, watching her join her friends.

"Her? That was--"

Thunder interrupted him before he could finish the sentence. I looked through the leaves; they were all bottom side up.

"Huh, maybe we should get down and get back inside," Bill said.

"You afraid of a little rain?" I asked, but my mind was still on the girl.

By the time the hail started, we were on the ground and sprinting to the house, with plans to meet up again the next day, but as we dodged the falling ice and the thunder that chased us to the door, I could not stop looking over my shoulder, wondering where that girl had gone.

And in this way, I met my best friend, and my father's career was launched, and we both had Owen Afton to thank for the whole thing.

Chapter 10:
The One-Eyed Moroccan

Nadia Lehcar Bin-Said sat surveying the city from the balcony of the room in the Rio de Janeiro Grand Hotel she called home. Although the cloud coverage had been moving in all day, on her nose rested large red sunglasses that hid the jagged scar on the left side of her face and her missing eye, the singular flaw on her strikingly beautiful face. She brought the long filter that held her cigarette to her thin, austere lips and took a deep drag. Her other hand rested on a large sapphire that hung from her neck. Out of the corner of her right eye, she could see a familiar man in uniform approaching the hotel.

There was a knock on her wooden door.

"Enter."

The door opened with a jolt. In the heat, it had swollen to barely fit its frame.

"Nadia." Officer Olan Oliveira greeted her.

"Ah, Olan," the Moroccan replied coolly.

"An American came to me today, and he reported the missing necklace of his wife. You wouldn't happen to know anything about this, would you?"

"I wish you wouldn't keep coming around my room with such baseless accusations, Olan." She blew smoke towards his face.

"Baseless, you say?"

"I haven't the slightest idea where that poor woman's necklace has gone, and if I did, you'd certainly be the first to know."

There was a silence in the room that hung between them. For five seconds, they eyed each other with curt intensity.

They burst into laughter. The jewel thief rose from her chair to greet her old friend with an embrace. She fixed them both some coffee.

"What a pleasure it is to see you, Olan, but must you always only stop by for business?"

"Many apologies my dear, but the city is abuzz with the Olympics coming up, and I did promise those Americans I'd find their necklace before they returned home."

She blew on her mug to cool off her coffee before taking a sip, casually massaging the jewels on her neck.

"Ah of course, and I certainly hope you do. As for the Olympics, how good for business do you expect the Games to be?"

"Oh excellent, I'm sure."

They clinked mugs and took a sip. The Jewel Thief and the Cop shared a view of Rio and a few sips of coffee before Olan Oliveira spoke up again.

"I can't stay long, I'm afraid. I have to meet with the American General Wertheim to speak about security for when their President arrives."

Nadia almost spilled her coffee as she was raising it to her lips. Immediately, she regained her composure.

"General what?"

"General Wertheim. Some pompous American who wants to tell me how to do my job."

Nadia was silent. Her hand was on her necklace again, and she looked out over Rio but saw none of the city. Olan took her silence as his cue to leave.

"A pleasure as always, Nadia. It will be a good few weeks for business. I look forward to it. Do try not to get caught?"

"I never do, Olan. Have a good day," she replied absentmindedly.

So Hunter is in town, she thought. *Perhaps I should…no.*

She shook her head and finished her coffee.

No. Years may pass but, some wounds never heal.

Nadia looked out over the city again with her one good eye.

She knew that all too well.

Chapter 11:
Ivana Carvalho

The Olympic Games were always an absolute nightmare for whomever happened to be the Minister of Health in the country they were held. Tourists and displaced peoples alike mingled together in an oppressing heat that always carried within it, disease. Ivana Carvalho had only recently been named the single youngest, and first female, *Ministério da Saúde* in the history of Brazil.

Ivana Carvalho used to sit in Mass with her husband Pedro, but now she sat alone.

"Mass" was a name for one hour every week where Catholics all gathered together in a room with painted windows to try and sing louder than the people next to them. Ivana was doing well this week, having not only out-sang her neighbors, but also out-dressed them as well; her face wore a tasteful, yet subtle, layer of makeup, her hair was pulled back into its usual tight bun, and a dress hung gracefully from her shoulders.

Her phone began to buzz in her purse. She looked around nervously, knowing, as all good Catholics do, that there is only a limited amount of room in Heaven. The competition to reach the pearly gates was a stiff one, and although no one was quite certain how to reach the Kingdom of the Lord for sure, Ivana knew you do not get there by taking calls in church; that much, at least, had been generally agreed upon.

Her phone kept on buzzing, either dismissive or disrespectful of the unforgiving Creator. Her neighbors were glancing towards her now with haughty disapproval etched on their faces.

"Merda," she swore, drawing further looks from her fellow churchgoers. Ivana grabbed her bag and strode out of the room at what she had decided was a discrete but dignified pace.

There were three missed calls to go along with one message that read: "URGENT. CALL BACK IMMEDIATELY." They were all from Jorge Suarez, a colleague of hers. Technically, he worked for her. Jorge had been studying the recent outbreak of a particularly virulent strain of a disease affecting local bats that the residents had taken to calling, appropriately, "Tadarida".

"Ivana? Where are you?"

"I'm at church, Jorge. I certainly hope that this is urgent," she said, although truthfully she hoped nothing of the sort.

"I'll skip the pleasantries, then. There is evidence that Tadarida can spread to humans."

Mass was letting out. All the children in their Sunday best were filing along with their families, on their way to different brunches and picnics and various family gatherings, passing behind Ivana. They all heard her swear.

"Ma'am?"

"Tell me, Jorge, do you have any good news for me at all?" she replied, striding through the church parking lot. "It is the Lord's day, after all."

There was silence at the other end of the line. The warm sun made Ivana squint, even through her heavy sunglasses. She wiped away beads of sweat from her forehead, beads that had nothing at all to do with the prodigious heat.

"Well, we currently are conducting further studies, but it could be containable."

"Could it?"

Ivana could hear Jorge's mind churning on the other end of the phone.

"We could certainly try. We just have yet to find out the precise way the disease transmits itself from host to host. We know mosquitoes spread it, but there is also evidence in lab tests that it has already begun to mutate. At the moment, we are trying to see if it might be able to be spread through water and air. Nothing is for certain yet."

The churchgoers were more scattered as they walked out of the doors, and their shadows on the ground were fewer and farther between.

It was such a beautiful day.

"It's your call, ma'am. Many of the athletes have already arrived but for those who haven't--"

"No. We can control this for one week, can't we? Besides, we don't even know the effects it may have on humans yet."

Jorge was quiet for so long that Ivana began to worry that he was no longer there.

"Jorge?"

"Right. Yes, of course, sorry. We'll get back to work, ma'am. God bless, Ivana."

"God bless you as well, Jorge."

The line went dead, and Ivana slowly lowered her phone, sighed, and lit her last cigarette. She would quit after this one. She meant it this time, it was taking too much of a toll on her teeth. Besides, it was a bad look to have a Minister of Health who was still a smoker.

Nine days. That's all they had until the whole thing was over. Nine days of tourists and chaos. After that she could focus on this Tadarida.

The tendrils of smoke climbed into the sky. The youngest, and last, Minister of Health in Brazil's history walked away from her church.

Chapter 12:
"Where Are You?"

"Do you ever think about how strange of a question that is?"

"What question?"

"Where are you?"

"How do you mean?"

"Well, it has to be a recent question, doesn't it?"

"I think it's existed for quite some time..."

"No, what I mean is that, our parents probably never asked that question even close to the amount of times that we do, right? They were either talking to someone face-to-face, sending a letter to a specific address, or they had to know exactly which phone to call to get in touch with who they wanted to talk to. Either way, they never really had to ask 'where are you,' did they?"

"No, I suppose they didn't."

"You should write about that."

"Write about what?"

"About how we never know where anyone else is anymore, about how it doesn't really even matter, but we still ask anyway."

Chapter 13:
Seventeen Days Ago

Seventeen days ago, I was sober. As it so happens, seventeen days ago my wife was also alive. Funny how those two things seem to match up like that.

Chapter 14:
El Niño

There is a natural phenomenon in the Pacific Ocean known as 'El Niño'. It is a weather pattern that occurs when the warm sea air of the southeast Pacific rises, creating a complex storm system that affects the weather patterns throughout the globe. It tends to be responsible for both widely spread and wildly varying weather phenomena, causing heavy rainfall in some areas of the world, while simultaneously being the cause of droughts in other regions. One of the areas that typically sees heavy rainfall during these episodes often seem to be South America, where the country of Brazil happened to be located. The rains would last for days, blanketing large swaths of the South American continent.

Now, as it happens, when an exceptionally large amount of rain falls onto a land that already experiences regular and intense rain falls, there can be, as a result, several negative side effects. Although the rain would eventually simply fade into the background of the everyday lives of the people of Brazil, the results of such intense and consistent rain periods were undeniable. Traffic accidents, for example, tend to rise dramatically during periods of heavy rain falls. Makeup runs, umbrella sales boom, and puddles form.

And puddles stay, in the warm wet heat where mosquitoes breed and spread, in a country blanketed by rain.

Ivana Carvalho removed her sunglasses. She had read somewhere recently that El Nino rains were making their way inland from the Pacific Coast, and that they could even settle in before nightfall. Ivana was quite alright with this, of course. The sunlight had been so bright all morning it had almost hurt her eyes. She was grateful it was receding as she stamped out the last tendrils of smoke from her cigarette and made her way out of the parking lot of her church.

The forecast called for rain.

Chapter 15:
The Church of Christ the Savior

At this point, I would like to pause for a moment to speak about the church of Ivana Carvalho.

In 1835, outside the city of São Paulo, Brazil, the slaves revolted. It started quietly, as all revolutions do, with one last injustice that shattered that illusion of impenetrable control.

"Out! Now, and single file."

The slaves walked down the splintered wooden plank from the ship to the sandy shore that burned against their bare feet. The men were chained to each other, the women and children in shackles to themselves. The sun was bright. It made them shield their eyes.

Being chained to one another made walking along the sand difficult. Some of them stumbled as orders continued to flow.

"Stand, you mulatto bastard!" barked a soldier, his boot making contact with the rib cage of a fallen child.

The child did not move.

When the soldier pulled back his foot to strike again, a woman dove to protect the boy. The soldier's foot did not stop, and with a crack the woman's nose was shattered.

A shout was raised from the men in chains. The woman on the ground wailed and dark blood gushed from her nose.

"Stay back and keep walking!" shouted the soldier, brandishing a whip in their direction. It was here, though, that he made his fatal mistake.

He turned his back to the woman.

Most people these days seem to have delusions of grandeur about the nature of a revolution. They imagine tall, strong generals sitting bravely on their white horses, calling the common man to arms.

These notions, though romantic, are all wrong. Revolutions are not started by men on horses. They are started by whispers in the darkness, shared like the chains that shackle down those who whisper for three long months, and ignited with raging fury by something as small and as simple as a fallen child, a sharp boot, a turned back.

The woman leaped from where she was and tackled the soldier to the ground. A second soldier shot her in the back, and all of a sudden, chaos erupted.

The slaves fought back against their captors, and when the sand and bullets settled, they found themselves still standing, living free in a strange land. The two boats that they had been brought over in from the ports of Angola sat groaning in their docks, so the newly freed men set about freeing the boats. They dragged these ships upon the land and overturned them, so that their hulls faced toward Heaven and their masts were snapped against the ground.

When the Portuguese stole these people from their homes in Africa, they did so in the name of God and gold, although it was clear to all which one they truly worshipped. The men and women who would not become slaves, though, found themselves entranced by the other. And so, from those two mammoth wooden ships, the ships that held benches and blood and powder and pain, where in chains they sat huddled not one day before, these now-free men built themselves a church. They filled the church with the benches that they traveled on, the ones that had been stained with their sweat and their blood, and the rows of pews to which they once were chained now stood in worship.

They had heard of stained glass but did not know how it was made, so they painted the windows of the ship with portraits of Mary and Joseph and Jesus himself, and named the church for Christ the Savior.

The pews of the church of Ivana Carvalho were worn slick from the centuries. This was the church she married Pedro in and the church in which she held his funeral; this was the church she sat in when her phone began to ring from Jorge Suarez, and where she learned about the bats.

Throughout the years, Ivana had noticed dark stains on some of the pews. They were splattered and faded, but every week, when she sat down to worship, she could not help but wonder what caused them. At one point, she had asked her pastor what they were from.

"Those stains are the blood of those who sailed across the ocean and freed themselves to build this church," he had said with reverence.

"And what happened to the Portuguese?"

"Well, they sent more men to Brazil with more slaves, but rebellions were starting to sprout up all throughout the continent, and the slave trade ended not long after."

Ivana pondered this for a moment before asking:

"So the slaves, did they ever go looking for the gold the Portuguese had come to find?"

"No, my child, I don't think they did, for they found a treasure far more valuable in their love for the Lord."

"Then the gold must still be out there!"

"Perhaps, perhaps not. But because of our ancestors' sacrifice, we have them to thank for this marvelous church."

Ivana liked this story and the thought that there may still be gold out in the Amazon rainforest somewhere. She thought about it every time she attended Mass.

Ivana would leave the church that day with her cigarette still smoldering in the parking lot. She would be back.

Chapter 16:
Frustration

"That chapter really stands out I think."

"What do you mean?"

"Why do you want to go so far on a deep dive of the church and its history?"

"I think it's a really interesting story."

"Is it true?"

"No. Yes. Not really."

"Then, why are you insisting on showing us the story of these early free Catholics?"

"I guess since I'm just a frustrated Catholic at my core, I like the stories of people who are in that boat with me."

"I don't think you're so alone there. I think a lot of the world are frustrated Catholics."

Chapter 17:
Drafted Theater

I often find that some of the best plays in the world are being performed in airport bars, on the Interstate Highway roads, in church parking lots, and all the other places where the Great American Theater is being played out.

One of my favorite places to watch the great show, though, was from the top of a parking garage. It seemed like everyone in the city was there just for me, acting out their parts with such utter conviction that they almost made me believe they were real. For the longest time, I would go alone and set my watch to the passing trains and see in vignettes the life of my city as it breathed in and let out a smoky sigh, all from my perch, alone on the dark side of the morning.

I thought I was the only one who could truly see the play for what it was.

I took her up with me one night. We gazed out on the city lights and watched as they flicked off, one by one.

We shared a cigarette above our city, and, as she leaned up against me, I whispered down to her hair, but not to her.

"The world is big and strange," I said.

"True," she said back to me, shifting her weight to reach up and pluck the cigarette right from my lips. "But at least it isn't lonely."

And, for the first time in my life, it wasn't.

Chapter 18:
General Hunter Wallace Warthog the Third

General Hunter Wallace Wertheim III was a military man raised by military men. Discipline, service, and unquestioning obedience to authority were of the utmost importance to him and to his father, Admiral Hunter Wallace Wertheim Jr. A commanding officer was never wrong in the Wertheim household. Junior was a Navy man, a rather significant factor in the Third's decision to join the Army instead.

His grandfather, his namesake and the original Hunter Wallace Wertheim, was, incidentally, a pacifist and communist sympathizer. He dabbled in anti-Korean War protests in the fifties and retired to a commune in New Mexico. Junior never told his son any of this, though, on account of familial pride being tremendously important to the Wertheim's.

General Hunter Wallace Wertheim III wore his crisp uniform as he approached the administration building on the São Paulo Army Base. In fact, he only ever wore Army-issued clothing; the only nonstandard-issue article of clothing he ever wore was a gold cross on a chain around his neck. He was forty-nine years old when he reached his rank, one of the youngest men ever to achieve the title of General. He earned his stripes in Israel, holding a tentative grip on the region for many years before being relocated to Brazil.

The position in Brazil had always struck those in the military world as a bit of a step down for Hunter Wallace Wertheim III, but he had not seemed to mind. In fact, he requested the transfer.

This, of course, did nothing to quell the rumors and whispers that had spread about his time in Israel. Never to his stern face, with its deep, tanned wrinkles and eyes as black as a shark's, but people did whisper about the woman, the one who escaped his custody, and left nothing but a small, golden cross behind her.

General Hunter Wallace Wertheim III walked briskly down a well-lit hallway, back straight and chest out, just like his father had taught him.

"You're a Wertheim, dammit," he would bark through clouds of cigarette smoke, "now walk like that name means something to you. Heel, toe, heel, toe, make it snap, Tripp!"

Throughout his entire adult life, Hunter Wallace Wertheim III never let anyone know that his parents had called him Tripp as a child.

"Hunter, don't be so hard on the boy, he's only six," Tripp's mother had said on many nights during his childhood.

"Without a little discipline, he'll never amount to anything!"

Junior shoved gruffly past his wife and turned back to his son.

"Not that you've got much of a shot as it stands anyway. There's no spine in you, is there, Tripp?" Junior had said, lighting up another cigarette.

Admiral Hunter Wallace Wertheim Jr. had passed away of cardiac arrest at the age of fifty-nine (incidentally, the same age as I am now). General Hunter Wallace Wertheim III never smoked a cigarette in his life.

The Third had lived at the São Paulo Army Base for the last nine years and entered his office on this rainy and humid August morning as he did so many mornings before and very, very few mornings after. The soft hum of the air-conditioning unit in the window and buzz of the fluorescent lights and mosquitoes were comfortable as he sat down behind his desk, attentive and invigorated with the energy that often accompanies an acute sense of purpose.

Being placed in charge of security detail for the most important man in the world, in a way, made you the most important man in the world, if you thought about it, and General Hunter Wallace Wertheim III had certainly thought about it quite a bit in the days that had led up to this one.

Today, the President of the United States arrived in Brazil, and the General had attention for this moment and this moment only. There were several manila folders neatly stacked to be ignored on his desk, all with CLASSIFIED stamped in red on the covers and labeled with boring titles like 'Israeli Protection Team' and 'Tadarida'. General Hunter Wallace Wertheim III knew better than to be distracted by these things with such an important event as the President's appearance at the Olympic Games resting on his squared-away shoulders.

The black phone on his desk rang. He picked up before it had finished its first ring.

"General Wertheim speaking."

"General Warthog? This is Ed Giaver, United States Secret Service."

General Hunter Wallace Warthog III paused for just a beat. This was a big moment for him, he knew that the President's arrival in Brazil relied on him.

"Right Ed, I'm here and ready."

"Well here's the thing Warthog." Ed's voice was fuzzy over the phone and General Warthog strained to pick up every word. "Here's the thing. We've heard some reports about tourists getting some sort of strange disease. We wanted to check in with you to make sure everything there is alright. Don't want the leader of the free world to be getting ill while at the Games, do we?"

Ed laughed with no humor, and the General could almost feel himself being analyzed through the receiver.

"I've heard similar things," Hunter Wallace Warthog replied, leaning against his desk, "but having spent the better part of a decade in this country, I can promise you it's no more than a bug, what with all these people packed in so close together. If it turns out to be anything more serious than a bout of the flu, I'd be shocked."

"That's exactly what we wanted to hear, Warthog, thanks for the intel. We'll keep you posted; touchdown should be within the next five hours."

"Sounds great Ed, looking forward to seeing Mr. President himself when he makes it in."

With a click, they hung up. General Hunter Wallace Warthog III gazed out his window. The rain had abated for the moment and the ground steamed around where the water pooled. He heard a faint buzzing around his head and slapped the back of his neck. A dead mosquito was there on his hand. He wiped it away with his tissue, preoccupied with rehearsing what his first words would be to the President of the United States of America. General Warthog III was going to meet the President.

If only his father could see him now.

Chapter 19:
Into the Village

Officer Olan Oliveira walked along the freshly paved asphalt road past rows of towers that shimmered, even in the rain. Ten high rises towered in a half circle, glass and concrete rising from the earth that still held the fresh bones of old favelas. They surrounded a pool, eight lanes wide and fifty meters long of crystal-clear water. The athletes were staying in these buildings with their respective nation's delegations; flags waved lazily from the balconies of almost every room, representing nearly every country in attendance, from Albania to Zimbabwe. Several of these athletes walked along the same path Olan was using now, as he approached his cadre of Officers to give his orders.

"Alright gents. Pretty straightforward. No one in or out."

A fresh-faced man in a newly pressed uniform raised his hand.

Olan sighed.

"Yes, Santos?"

"What about the athletes, sir?"

"Obviously I'm not talking about the athletes, Santos. Does anyone else have any questions?"

Nobody else raised a hand. They stood, shoulder to shoulder, at attention in the mist.

"Alright. We'll be working in shifts. Santos, switch with Silva and take the first shift off. I think you need some sleep."

There was chuckling, and Santos stepped back with glowing cheeks. An unfortunate move on his part; it put him just within arm's reach of Silva, who smacked Santos on the back of the head.

"As for the rest of you, you know your posts. Let's get to work."

The men dispersed, elbowing Santos in the ribs as they went. Oliveira shook his head, but the corners of his lips were curled up beneath his pencil-thin mustache, as much as he tried to hide the grin. He began his patrol.

Around him, through the mist, walked the greatest physical specimens that mankind had ever been able to offer. Although the rain persisted, so did the heat, and the faces of the athletes ran with rivulets of sweat that were indistinguishable from the mist that too soaked their chiseled cheeks; it gave them a gleam, an appearance of something otherworldly.

Demigods, on their very own Olympus.

Suddenly, Olan felt as if he was an intruder. Unworthy. He stood a little bit straighter, and his strides grew longer and somehow more deliberate.

A Jamaican sprinter emerged from the mist, walking next to a gymnast from somewhere in Eastern Europe; Olan could not quite place the colors. He was tall and lanky and, as far as Oliveira could tell, did not possess a shred of fat on his body. The gymnast who walked with him resembled something of a lynx and moved with the grace of one. Each step she took seemed as though it had never quite touched the ground before the next one started. The two were pantomiming something to each other that made Olan blush. They faded back into the mist behind the Officer as he walked on.

He passed the pool and the track that went around it. The water was pristine and filled with giants of men and women. The strokes they took were leisurely, but they moved through the water with such ease and grace that they may have been the sons and daughters of Neptune himself.

Two Americans were swimming breaststroke in lanes next to each other, matching each other stroke for stroke down the pool. A young boy was swimming not too far behind them. The other swimmers had stopped to watch this display of skill and power. Olan had as well.

The two touched the wall simultaneously. They came up breathing heavily and patting each other on the back. The boy touched not far behind, but he came up coughing. A burly man with thick hair covering his forearms and a Coach's badge hanging from his neck came over to the young man. He had the gait of someone who had once been an extraordinary athlete but had taken to retirement with enthusiasm and gusto. He still had his strength, though, and with ease he helped pull the boy out of the water. The coach tossed his swimmer a towel and barked at him with force in Hungarian. Olan did not speak the language but could make out words that sounded like 'Technique!' and 'Focus!' Olan did not think that the boy was paying attention; he had not stopped coughing since he had touched the wall. Slowly, Olan turned from the pool to face back down the new road.

Olan walked on through the mist and this village of gods, continuing his patrol.

Chapter 20:
The Opening Ceremonies

Sarah Pulski and Natalie Way were elbowed repeatedly maneuvering through the screaming crowd as they shoved their way into the central stadium in Rio de Janeiro for the Opening Ceremonies of the 2016 Olympics.

They moved with the crowd, more like caught leaves in a stream than human beings with deliberate actions; the collective swell of bodies pushed them forward.

Sarah and Natalie were wearing their Team USA shirts and had each purchased a commemorative hat. The two women were of similar height, and, save for Natalie's deeply tanned skin and dyed blonde hair, could almost be taken for sisters. Sarah's bright green eyes ate up the spectacle all around them, peering between shoulders to get a better glimpse of the field and ceremonies below. Natalie was much more focused on reaching their seats.

"It says here we still have to go up another level!" Natalie shouted.

Sarah nodded, more an acknowledgment that her friend had said anything at all than any sort of true agreement.

So they climbed the stairs to where their vantage point gave them a view of the entire production, and, although they were far from the scene themselves, they could observe the twirl of every last flamenco dancer.

"Oh, fuck me," Natalie said, staring at their seats, her cheeks flushed and breath ragged.

In their seats sat two Brazilian men.

"Hey. Hey! You two, up!"

The drunk man and his friend prattled to each other in rapid Portuguese, pretending not to notice the loud American woman until Natalie jabbed a finger into his shoulder. He looked up.

"Are you listening? Get up!"

"Ay, we were here first!"

"Yeah, but did you buy these tickets, motherfuckers?"

"Natalie!"

The drunker man whispered something in his friend's ear and they rolled into laughter.

"I'm sorry, is there something funny to you?"

"If you want to sit, you're more than welcome to sit in my lap."

"Oh like fuck did he just say that to me."

Natalie lunged, keys in hand, and it was all Sarah could do to hold her back.

By the time the men sitting in Sarah and Natalie's seats stood and, with reproachful eyes, walked their own way out of the row, they each had been scratched along their face and were bleeding from their cheeks.

The two women finally sat down.

The procession had already begun.

"Sarah, do you see the dancers?"

But Sarah was already staring in awe at the spectacle before them; she barely heard a thing Natalie had said.

The Brazilian Olympic Planning Committee had been tasked with putting on display, for the largest audience the world had ever seen, an extravaganza unlike anything in modern human history.

Dancers and fireworks lit the night with colors, and Sarah and Natalie sat, completely enthralled. It was as though some old god of light and color had awoken and now gripped the night and the city and the people in his spell.

The countries began to march out their athletes and coaches. Brazil, the host, led the parade, and the demigods of the modern world marched to the music of their homelands. Some countries, like Mauritania, could only field one or two athletes. Some, like Spain, were fielding hundreds. Sarah had never heard of some of the places like Bhutan and Seychelles, but she roared when the United States presented their delegation, with Kevin Adrian strutting at the head of the crowd, American flag held high.

The ceremonies lasted for over four hours, but if Sarah had been asked, she would have said either four minutes or four full, sunlit days. It had gone by in a blink, but she could have sworn she had always lived in that moment.

They were caught in the swell again as they left the stadium, fighting for the last cabbie who spoke a lick of English. They were nearly shaking with the energy that stayed with them from the Opening Ceremonies. The adrenaline that was still pumping when they got back to the hotel may have been part of the reason Natalie almost fought the driver when she saw him upcharge them as they drove up to the front door. Sarah paid with cash and ushered Natalie back inside, but even this altercation was not enough to keep the conversation off of the Olympic Games for long.

"Did you even know that a place such as Saint Lucia existed?"

Sarah and Natalie were staying in a hotel an hour drive from downtown Rio de Janeiro. They had saved up for years, since the location of the games had been announced all the way back when they were still in high school together, for the opportunity to come to Brazil for the opening ceremonies. They had gotten the hotel room on the cheap. It was a small place, with dark parquet floors and a single lamp by the wall. There was not a right angle to be had in the entire room.

They were stripping their sweat-stained Team USA T-shirts off their backs. The lack of air conditioning did nothing to dampen their spirits. Sarah was the first to wash herself with the frigid water from their doorless bathroom.

She called from the bathroom to her friend. Her voice was muffled from behind the towel she was using to dry herself off.

"I've got an Aunt Lucia. At least, I think I do. We never saw much of my mom's side of the family. Fucking hell that's cold. You're up!"

"That cold, huh? Well, aren't I excited now."

Natalie traded places with Sarah in the bathroom.

"Some of those athletes looked so young though, didn't they, Nat?"

"Oh Christ, didn't they? Who was that one boy? The one from Honduras?"

"No, it wasn't Honduras. Hungary, I think it was."

"Ah, that's right. God, he couldn't've been a day over fifteen!"

"I don't think they let 'em in that young, Nat."

"Still though," said Natalie, leaning her head out of the doorframe while drying her hair, "makes you think about our own lives a bit, doesn't it?"

"How do you mean?"

"Well, what were we doing when we were fifteen?"

"He's not fifteen, Nat!"

"Fine, then, seventeen! Whatever!" Natalie said, with more than a hint of exasperation as she lay down on the bed. "Were you dating Bill by then?"

"Jesus, it's hard to remember a time when I wasn't dating Bill."

"Oh, don't tell me it's bad again?"

"Honestly, Nat? I don't think I've been in love with him since high school. It's like--"

Sarah was interrupted by a bout of coughing. She raised her eyebrows at her friend.

"Jesus, girl. Are you sure you don't want to get that looked at?"

"Nah, I'll be alright. There must be something in the air here."

"I heard other people coughing at the stadium tonight."

"Yeah, well, I feel like I always get sick while I'm traveling. Do you think we're allowed to smoke in the room?"

"Seriously? You think that's a good idea?"

But Natalie had already lit up one of the dark Brazilian cigarettes she had picked up on their way back to the hotel. "Ah, now I feel better. What were you saying?"

Sarah laughed and shook her head. Her hair was still drying so she tied it up above her head. "Forget it. What's the plan for tomorrow?"

"Well, our flight is pretty late, so we have the chance to catch some of the earlier swimming events, or maybe, a boxing match or something."

"Yeah, that sounds good to me." As she yawned, she lay back down on her side of the queen bed they would be sharing. "I'm feeling pretty wiped out, Nat. I may hit the hay."

Natalie put her cigarette out on the alarm clock sitting on the nightstand and lay back too. The last thing Sarah noticed before dozing off was the skin around Natalie's eyes. It seemed vaguely more yellow to Sarah than she had ever noticed on her friend's face before.

Sarah would hardly get a good night's sleep. Natalie's coughing would keep her up nearly throughout the entire night as they lay in their humid room in Brazil. All throughout the country, people were beginning to cough.

Chapter 21:
Stardust

"Everyone in this story feels very lonely."

"What makes you say that?"

"I don't know, they just feel so isolated. From themselves, from each other, they all just seem very alone."

"I think I know what you mean, like that feeling when you look at the stars sometimes?"

"You feel lonely when you look at the stars?"

"Yeah, don't you? It makes me feel so small and insignificant."

"But we're made of the stuff that comes from the stars! You shouldn't feel lonely when you see them, you should feel at home."

"Up against all that, we're basically just dust, aren't we?"

"Stardust."

"Is there any difference?"

"...I think so. I think there has to be."

Chapter 22:
The Absent and the Absinthe

"Albi, darling, when was the last time you opened a window in here?"

Ivana stepped gingerly over empty containers of liquor and paint mingled indiscriminately on the floor of the dark apartment.

"And when was the last time you went outside?"

"Ah Ivana, good morning, my love," the little man's voice was muffled in the hazy room from behind a large canvas.

"It's five in the afternoon, Albi. But yes, good morning to you as well."

Albi de Foix's windows were drawn with stained sheets, and the light streamed yellow into the room, cutting through the smoke and dust that floated through the air. He stumbled forward and swore as he tripped over an empty decanter.

"What brings you here on this fine morning, Ivana?"

"The members of the Olympic Planning Committee know that you and I are friends, so they have asked me to speak with you on their behalf."

"Ah, those pretentious bastards, making demands and calling me nonstop. What do they want now?"

"They want their mural, Albi."

"Why would they want the mural? The Olympics are not for weeks."

"The Olympics started two days ago, and they paid you upfront."

"Pah! I know when the Olympics started Ivana, do you take me for a fool?"

Albi stood to his full height of 4'1" and walked to his kitchen to rummage through some cabinets and find a not-quite-yet-empty bottle of absinthe.

"How can you stomach that stuff?"

"It reminds me of home." Albi grimaced as he swallowed. "Although the swill you get on this side of the Atlantic almost makes me want to go back. Tell the Planning Committee that I could never finish the mural."

Albi de Foix was born and raised in rural France, where he was viewed as somewhat of a local freak. He was abandoned by his parents and raised by the nuns of a convent outside of the port city of Le Havre. He was a troubled child. Albi was frequently found tearing the illustrated pages from the books in the library and, when he was older, in the Chapel cabinet with empty bottles of Communion wine. The small chapel where the nuns worshipped was Albi de Foix's universe; it was the one part of the convent he did not attempt to destroy in any way. He would spend hours tracing the stained-glass windows, but whenever one of the Sisters attempted to view, let alone frame, his tracings, he hid or tore or burned them. Even so, it was not long before he began to be known as something beyond a terror and a freak; a child prodigy.

From a young age, word of his immense talent as a painter began to spread like wildfire. He grew renowned in the art community for his impossible to purchase pieces of art. What manifested itself as extremely high demand, however, was in reality due to Albi's absolute refusal to put any paintings for sale on the market. This resulted in his constantly being pursued by collectors, looking to offer him exorbitant sums of money in exchange for just a few sketches. The few works of his that did make it to market were largely nicked from his studio while he was in a drunken stupor; half-finished paintings of surreal landscapes and sketched portraits only partially painted in. These were among the most sought after pieces of art on the modern market, and only pushed

Albi further into isolation. He began to move from country to country, leaving after the collectors caught up to him again, until he crossed the Atlantic and moved into a flat not too far down the street from Brazil's brand-new Minister of Health, Ivana Carvalho, the first person of repute he began to interact with that did not try to push him to sell her his art.

"Did you burn all the drafts again?"

"They were not satisfactory!" Albi yelled as he returned to his canvas.

Ivana rolled her eyes and accepted the glass of absinthe handed her way. She placed it on a crowded table beside her as Albi de Foix returned to his canvas, with his glass in one hand and his brush in the other.

"You know, Albi, one of these days you're actually going to have to finish one of your paintings for you to be a true genius."

"I have finished many paintings, Ivana, just not my masterpiece! Not yet, anyway."

"Not the mural, either."

"Not the mural."

Albi had been commissioned by the Olympic Planning Committee to paint a commemorative mural to be displayed at the closing ceremonies of the 2016 Olympic Games. He would never quite complete what the Committee had in mind, but, one day soon, he would indeed complete his masterpiece.

"I'll tell them you're still working on it then?"

"Tell them they'll get it when the Games begin!"

Ivana sighed.

"One day, Albi, my friendship with you will be the death of me."

"Oh, are we friends? Because it certainly seems like to me, Ivana, that all you've come to see me about was business."

"Don't you pull that with me, Fox! It's all I could do to keep the dogs off your back for this long."

It was true. Ivana had flexed her connections as far as they would go, but even governmental bureaucracy has its limits when it comes to inefficiency, and the French painter had finally found them. Albi spat on the floor and muttered under his breath something about the damn dogs in French, although, it lightened his mood considerably to hear Ivana refer to them in such a way.

"Won't you stay and have another drink with me, darling?" Albi asked, oblivious to the still full glass on the table beside him.

"I can't. I'm expecting a call from Jorge at any moment, and the swimming preliminary rounds are already underway. I really ought to be going quite soon."

As Albi de Foix began to reply, Ivana's phone buzzed to life.

"Excuse me, Albi, this is Jorge now. With good news, I hope. I must take this."

And so Ivana Carvalho stepped outside, and Albi de Foix returned to his canvas yet again and began to paint.

"No no no, much too bright. There needs to be something darker." He spoke aloud as his brush moved furiously from palate to canvas. He hardly noticed the pale white of Ivana's face when she reentered the dingy apartment, nor the shaking of her hands as she slowly closed the door.

"Ah, Ivana, good morning my love." The little man's voice was muffled in the hazy room as he called from behind the large canvas.

"I must be going, Albi."

"Won't you stay for a drink?" the little man called.

Ivana Carvalho swallowed the entire glass of absinthe in one go.

"No, my dear. There is somewhere I must go," she replied. "Best of luck on your masterpiece."

Albi spoke, although not to her, as the door of the French painter shut behind Ivana again for the last time.

"Yes," he muttered, his brush flying, "something darker. That's much better."

Chapter 23:
Something Darker

Sarah Freeman, formerly Sarah Pulski, was the second person in the continental United States to display symptoms of the Tadarida virus.

The first was Natalie Way.

The plane had taken off from Rio de Janeiro, Brazil, with the final destination being Cleveland, Ohio, with a two hour stop in Houston, Texas.

Sarah took her seat, next to the window. Every person who walked by her had beads of sweat on their forehead; Natalie kept walking by and wiped her brow.

"How can an airplane be this hot?"

"Well, I guess that's just Brazil, right?" Sarah replied.

"God, to think I was just starting to like the place."

They took their seats squarely in the middle of the main cabin, with Sarah next to the window and Natalie sitting in the middle, resigned to spending the next fifteen hours some thirty-thousand feet in the air. As the plane began to pressurize, the window started to develop a layer of mist. In front of Sarah sat a mother and her young child. Behind her sat a priest, and up near the front there was an older, well-dressed man sitting next to a woman who must have been thirty years his junior.

Sarah wondered if he was her father until she saw her kiss him.

"Jesus, can you believe that, Nat?"

"Hmm? What happened?"

"Those two up there! That old guy and the girl?"

"Fuck, no way, you can't be serious?"

Natalie's eyes were wide as she peered to get a better look. Sarah grabbed Natalie's shoulder and shoved her back down into her seat.

"Stop it, they'll see us!"

"Do you think he bought her?"

"Natalie!"

"What!"

Sarah laughed and looked out onto the tarmac. The plane was finally starting to take off. Sarah traced her name in the mist on the window. First *Sarah Pulski*. Then, below that, she began to write *Sarah Freeman*, but before she had reached the *m*, the plane was in the air and the mist faded rapidly away, taking her name with it. Natalie coughed.

"Jesus, you need to get that checked out."

"Nah, I think it's just something in the air."

The mother in front of them coughed as well.

"Looks like you're not the only one who came down with something here."

But as Sarah jested, she began to notice that other people in the cabin were also coughing.

"You excited to see the hubby?"

"I guess. I hope he hasn't killed Seymour by now. It just… it was nice to get away, you know?"

"That bad?"

Sarah shifted in her seat.

"I'm not sure we're doing anything more than going through the motions at this point. I don't even know if I love him anymore."

"Well fucking leave his ass then! You can move in with me. I've got a nice couch."

"You've had that couch for like seven years, Natalie, and it was in your parent's basement for like twenty. I wouldn't sleep on it if you paid me to."

"Whatever, you get my point. Think about it."

The fasten seatbelt light had turned off and flight attendants began to pass out the meals. They got to Sarah and Natalie quickly.

"Will that be the chicken or the beef?"

They both looked the same shade of grey to Sarah. "Chicken."

The priest was coughing.

"There must be something wrong with the air in here," he said to no one in particular.

Sarah shivered and pulled an itchy blanket out of a plastic bag, the one the airline had provided. It was thin, and she could hardly tell she even had it on. Why was she so cold? How did it get this cold after being boiling hot?

The old man coughed, and the woman with him looked almost hopeful to Sarah.

She began coughing too.

"It looks like everyone is starting to get sick," Sarah said.

The small child's cough was high-pitched.

"There must be something wrong with the air in here, right?" the mother turned around. "Do you think that's it? Is it the plane? We didn't feel sick until we got on it."

Sarah and Natalie looked at each other.

"Well, I mean, I was coughing a little bit before we got on," said Natalie.

"Wait, are you the one getting everyone sick?"

The priest had overheard this exchange.

"It can't be her. I was coughing before I got on as well."

"So it's both of you!" The mother's voice was raising.

A flight attendant approached their section.

"Excuse me, ma'am, is something wrong?"

"Yes! These two here are infecting the whole cabin! They need to be--"

She was interrupted by a barking cough from the flight attendant herself. The mother's eyes seemed to grow twice in size to Sarah.

"Oh my god. It's all of you. It's this airplane! The air in the airplane is making people sick!"

By now, the attention of the entire cabin had turned to these women.

"Ma'am," the flight attendant began, "I'm going to have to ask you to sit down and lower your voice."

The mother looked very much like she was prepared to do anything but that, but before she could answer, a voice was raised from the back.

"Hey, I think she's right! We deserve to know why everyone is sick in here!"

"Yeah! What's happening on this plane? Why is everyone coughing?"

Their voices were rising, like a swelling tide, like the fever they didn't know they already had.

The truth was that every person in that cabin had already been infected, and some of them were starting to show it. Most of them were infected even before they stepped foot on the plane, and those that weren't, had received their disease simply while sitting on the tarmac. The virus was already coursing through their veins; there was nothing at all that the flight attendants could do to help them, particularly because they were all beginning to fall ill themselves. So, naturally, they were the first ones to be blamed for the outbreak. They already had fear behind their eyes, and voices that were breaking when they called for calm.

"People! Please, let's settle down so we can figure out what's going on!"

"We already know what's going on! You got us all sick!" shouted a red-faced man from the back.

Sarah and Natalie tried to shrink from the confrontation.

The Fasten Seatbelt light came on.

"They're trying to silence us because they know we're right!"

Sarah whispered to Natalie, "Why won't that guy shut up?"

A voice came through the intercom.

"Ladies and gentlemen, this is your captain speaking. I understand there's been a bit of a disturbance in the main cabin. We are trying to sort everything out, but in the meantime, if you all could take your seats, that would help us out a lot."

Eventually, after much coaxing, most of the passengers took their seats and, with the exception of the coughing, quiet fell over the cabin.

The coughing, echoing over the travelers like some bizarre melody, kept the cabin from falling into true silence. The hacking. It had spread to everyone, and by the time they landed, not one person was spared from the gut-wrenching cough.

When they arrived at the Cleveland Hopkins International Airport, coughing as they collected their bags, Cleveland, Ohio, did not yet know what they were about to do, but it was certainly about to feel the impact.

By the time Sarah arrived back to her home and discovered the note to her husband, they had already infected nearly every passenger on their flight, not to mention the several dozen other people they had interacted with on their way out of the airport. These people would, in turn, go on to infect their families and friends and taxi drivers, who would go on to spread the disease further, and so on and so forth, as diseases go.

By the next morning, roughly 12 percent of Cleveland, Ohio, had come in contact with Tadarida, and the airplanes leaving from Hopkins had begun to spread it to many other major metropolitan areas.

Chapter 24:
The Cough and the Cop

Officer Olan Oliveira shook his pen to free up some ink.

"So please, again sir, can you explain to me what happened?"

The Spanish tourist coughed into his hand outside of the Olympic Aquatic Center. He was overweight and carrying a Spanish flag, furiously polishing his glasses with his shirt. His wife sat on the curb behind him, eyes darting with apprehension around the crowd. Olan sighed with impatience and glanced around at the chattering group of tourists that surrounded them. The rain had slowed down to just a vague mist, and people from all over the world were waving the flags of their home countries. Even though it seemed that only the same four or five countries were the ones to win events, it still made everyone quite pleased with themselves to display the colors of their homeland.

The man placed the glasses back on his face and blinked hard several times.

"Officer, we were just standing there, and then my wife's purse was suddenly gone."

"Right. Did you get a look at who took it?"

"I…darling, did you see who took it?" The Spanish man looked at his wife.

She shook her head.

Olan pretended to write something down before looking up and around again. The mist was thick, unseasonably so. It clouded the man's glasses and he took them off to again clear them with his shirt.

The cop took a closer look at the crowd this time. He was on edge. Something seemed off. The man kept talking as Officer Oliveira scanned their surroundings. He could only see so far before the shapes faded into the grey. The muffled sounds from the swim arena echoed thickly through the various patriotic supporters, excited to see their homeland's favorite sons and daughters compete. It sounded as though a new race was to begin shortly.

"Excuse me, Officer, are you listening to me?"

He wasn't.

"Yes, of course I am. Do you know when exactly this took place?"

"It couldn't have been more than half an hour ago."

The air was warm despite the mist. Olan folded up his notepad and placed it into his breast pocket.

"The trouble is that anyone could have taken it, and my men are spread thin enough as it is. I haven't the faintest idea what you expect me to do about a missing purse."

"Look for it!"

"I suggest the lost and found, sir, but I will certainly keep an eye out for it."

The inspector left the man sputtering to his wife in Spanish. He turned around and walked through the crowd and the mist.

Now, though, Olan could see what was wrong; the coughing. As he made his way through the crowd, the ubiquity of the illness grew only more evident. He was there for security, and perhaps to serendipitously assist wealthy tourists locate their missing treasures, but he could not help but feel a sense of unease about this new development.

The speakers in the plaza announced that the long-anticipated race between Andrew Cordes and Kevin Adrian was about to get underway. Olan shook his head and continued his patrol.

Chapter 25:
No Safe Sins

"Of course you wanted a scene in the mist."

"What's wrong with the mist?"

"Nothing, it's just too… poetic."

"And you have a problem with that?"

"Let me just say this; if you ever write me in the mist, I may just have to kill both of us then and there."

"I promise you, then, here and now, that I'll never write you in the mist."

"Yes, you will. You'll write me there eventually."

"Don't you believe me?"

"I love you, darling, but no sin with you is safe."

Chapter 26:
The Hungarian

On the fourth day of the Olympic Games in 2016, the breaststrokers, representing the absolute peak of human physicality, stood up on their blocks to a thunderous applause. Attention was, naturally, focused on lanes four and five, for they contained the two greatest breaststroke swimmers mankind had ever produced. Andrew Cordes and Kevin Adrian were about to fight each other in what may have been the single greatest athletic competition of all time; four years of training boiled down to a world's record-shattering 56.45 seconds for Cordes, edging out a 56.46 from Adrian. It was truly spectacular and absolutely ought to be regarded as an ultimate feat of human athletic triumph.

Of course, no one would ever remember that battle of extraordinary talent. This was because in lane seven, the Hungarian teenager, Devlin Gergely, the surprisingly young contender in an otherwise veteran race, made a much, much larger mark on human history when he promptly died in the middle of the pool.

Two days before the race, Devlin had begun to exhibit flu-like symptoms. A cough, some nausea, enough to be noticed by his longtime coach. When he was approached about his health, however, he insisted on racing, due to the fact that he had trained his entire life for this singular event and was not going to miss it on account of some stupid bug, dammit.

The day before the finals were the qualifying heats. Although he would never tell anyone this, and although he swam a Hungarian national-record-setting time, from the time he hit the water to the time he touched the wall, he could not recall a single stroke, kick, or turn. He had heard stories about athletes getting into a zone where they lose all sensory relations and operate on such a physically extreme level that they forget all the pain of the exertion. He assumed that this was what he had experienced.

Unfortunately, he was not remotely correct.

What he was actually experiencing was the deterioration of his nervous system. In truth, he was already dead; from that moment on, there was no way modern medicine could possibly save him. However, because of his superb physical condition and intense will to compete, he had one day left in him that he could push through.

Six hours before the race, Devlin experienced a coughing fit that left him heaving for air. He did not tell his coach.

Three hours before the race, Devlin began to swim laps in the warm-up pool. Waves of nausea overcame him. His coach told him it was likely just the nerves and gave him water to drink. Devlin thanked his coach and continued swimming.

One hour before the race, the nausea had turned agonizing. Devlin vomited in the state-of-the-art locker room near the racing pool. A thick, black bile fell from his mouth, along with two of his teeth. He exited the locker room to prepare for the race. His brain was too racked with fever to make anything resembling a rational decision.

Fifteen minutes before the race, he did not notice his childhood hero and inspiration, Andrew Cordes, extend a handshake for good luck. After holding it there for several moments, Andrew awkwardly returned to his own place in the clerk-of-course (the small room where all the breaststrokers were placed before the race).

Two minutes before the race, Devlin looked pale behind the blocks, but hardly any eyes were on him, as the legendary Cordes/Adrian feud was ready and set to fire off into the water.

He dove in at the whistle, mechanically flawless. Truly, an incredible dive. Devlin had always been good at starts.

Ten seconds into the race, Devlin was fifteen meters down the pool and slowing. Something was clearly wrong. Andrew Cordes and Kevin Adrian were already a body length ahead of world-record pace.

Twenty-three seconds into the race and Devlin reeled in the water, trailing far behind Cordes and Adrian, and everyone else for that matter, gulping for air, getting only water, and retching up the thick, black bile.

Devlin Gergely passed away exactly forty-nine seconds into the final heat of the hundred-meter breaststroke in the 2016 Olympic Games.

Andrew Cordes and Kevin Adrian celebrated their remarkable performances alone, as they were the only two people in the world not watching Devlin Gergely's body being pulled from the water by three lifeguards.

One of whom was coughing.

In the stands, the President of Brazil looked over at his Minister of Health. She did not notice though. Her gaze was for the pool alone, staring, enraptured, in horror.

Three rows to her left the President of the United States was already being surrounded by his bodyguards. A rigid-looking general sitting behind him began to cough and, looking down at his hand, saw speckles of something dark and thick.

Chapter 27:
Bella Donna

From her room's balcony, Nadia could usually see the entire Olympic Games' campus. There was the Village, where the athletes were housed during the hours when they were not competing, and off to the right were the swimming facilities.

Nadia's long cigarette filter dangled from her thin fingers. Tendrils of smoke drifted and mingled indiscriminately with the mist. Despite the overcast weather conditions, Nadia wore her large red sunglasses as she peered down over the crowd below as she thought of Olan and the hassle he must be dealing with far below her. She absentmindedly ran her fingers over the large sapphire that was the centerpiece of her necklace.

Her mind was decades away from her, back thinking of Israel, when she had first met her love, an American man named Hunter.

She had arrived there when she was still a young woman, chased east from Morocco by soldiers and the wealthy oligarchs that funded them. She arrived in Tel Aviv with nothing to her name but a bag full of stolen jewels.

Nadia had been on the run nearly all her life. Her father had been arrested when she was a child. When the military police came to take him away, they taunted the young girl in the home. They were going to sell her; she looked to be almost twelve years old, and some businessman could always use a new wife.

They stopped laughing when she bit the nearest one's arm. She tore out a chunk of flesh before he sliced her down the face with the blade that was strapped to his leg; bleeding and dodging potshots fired from the window, she ran and never looked back.

She had wandered throughout Northern Africa for years, taking what was not nailed down and leaving a bit of a name for herself; the gorgeous one-eyed Moroccan thief who had a keen eye for jewels. She was already rather infamous by the time she set foot in Tel Aviv.

She drew looks when she entered the bar called Satchmo on the banks of the Mediterranean Sea. The warm sea breeze brushed through the open window and filled the bar with the smell of salt. The walls were painted with murals of the coast, palm trees and golden sunsets, giving the illusion of a continued, unified beach, stretching from the sandy shallows up to the risen platform stage in the rear. A jazz band was playing to the small crowd of locals.

The women showed no outward signs of their wretched impropriety. They were dressed in a fashion that would have made the men in Morocco shudder in shame; short skirts and white tops were ubiquitous, they held alcohol in their hands that they had bought themselves, without a father or brother or husband there to supervise them.

She sat at the bar, apprehensive of the suspicious gazes of those who sat near her. They seemed to be eyeing her bag.

The woman next to her stood with her friends and walked away, leaving behind her purse. Nadia immediately picked it up.

She felt someone's rough and calloused hand suddenly grip her wrist.

"That is not yours." A man with a deep voice accused her.

"She left it, so she must not care about it anymore."

"That's not how things work around here, darling."

"It is how the world works everywhere. If you care about something, you must keep it close. Anything you leave behind you, you must be prepared to lose."

She struggled to loosen her wrist from the man's grasp. "If you think otherwise, you must be horribly naïve, darling!"

To Nadia's surprise and frustration, the man chuckled.

"I'll tell you what; I'll trade you your wrist for the bag."

Reluctantly, Nadia capitulated, handed the bag over, and looked her captor up and down. He was quite handsome. He wore a flattop haircut and held a flawless posture, that of a soldier; she recognized it immediately. How a soldier held himself was a dead giveaway to a woman on the run.

He was not Moroccan, but that alone did not quell all of her suspicions as she turned back to the bar. He had cold, dark eyes that did not seem to smile when he flashed his teeth towards her.

"American?" she asked.

The man motioned to the bartender that all was well.

"How can you tell?"

She scoffed. "You're not serious, are you? You make it painfully obvious."

"I can see you're not exactly from here yourself."

"Very observant of you."

"Can I buy you a drink?"

Nadia was taken aback. She gathered herself.

"If you must."

They waited for the drinks to arrive, and the American glanced down and saw Nadia's luggage.

"What's in the bag?"

She slid it farther beneath her stool with her foot.

"That is no business of yours."

"And what happened to your eye?"

"You know, I've changed my mind. I don't need that drink," she turned to leave. She felt a hand grab her wrist again and looked at him with anger flashing in her one good eye.

"Grab my wrist again, and that will be the last time you grab anything."

He let her go and she stood.

"Hold on a second," he said.

"What?"

"Do you even have a place to stay?"

She looked at him but did not see any malice in his eyes. Just a poor, simple soldier looking for company.

In other words, an easy mark.

"No."

"Do you want one?"

"Do you have a cigarette?"

The American made a face. "Never touched them."

"Buy me some, and let's take a walk."

They left the bar and meandered down the shore with the moon overhead. Nadia took a deep pull from her cigarette and closed her eye as she let the first hit of the dark Israeli nicotine fill her lungs.

"Are you here for work?" the American asked her.

"In a sense…"

The Moroccan stopped walking and removed her shoes. The sun had been down for hours, but the sand was still warm against her feet. She strolled out into the warm water that lapped her ankles, and, for a moment, the crimes of her father and the soldiers who were chasing her seemed miles away, not on her shoulders like they always had been. She had never felt so free. She had almost forgotten what it was like to feel safe.

"What do you go by?"

Nadia thought for a moment.

"Bella Donna," she answered.

"Hunter Wertheim," he joined her in the water and extended a calloused hand.

"What are you doing here, Hunter?"

"I'm stationed here to help keep the peace. We're doing weapons training with the Israeli Army."

"That does not sound to me as though there is much peace to be kept."

"For as long as I'm here, there will be."

Nadia laughed. "Best of luck to you, then, Hunter-the-peace-keeper. I suspect you may need it." She offered him the cigarette.

He withdrew without thinking.

"Right, I forgot, never touching the cigarettes. Why is that?"

"My father was always a big smoker."

"As was mine, but that hasn't kept me from them."

"Maybe you are closer with your father than I was with mine," he grumbled to the surf.

"Oh? Has your father passed?"

"Yesterday. That's why I was at the bar. Having a drink to celebrate."

"You dishonor your father so?"

Nadia's surprise betrayed her.

"Trust me, it's the only way anyone who knew him should react."

"One way or another, Hunter-the-peace-keeper," Nadia said softly, her one eye gazing now, not at the American but rather at the reflection of the moon in the warm, briny waves, "we are all what our fathers make us."

It was the early morning now, and Hunter was asleep in his bed in the barracks of the American Army base. Nadia lay awake, covered only by a coarse blanket, waiting for his breathing to become deep and regular. When she was certain he was in the deepest depth of sleep, she silently stood from bed, slipped into her dress, and got to work.

She knelt at the foot of the bed and began to dig through Hunter's bag. Nadia pulled the cash from his wallet and slipped his watch into her bag. She made her way to his door. Her hand was on the handle when she stopped; there was a brief pause in the American's regular droning snores. She looked back at him, as he murmured in his sleep and turned over.

Nadia could never say what caused her to do what she did next, but as she watched him sleep, she let go of the door handle, slipped off her dress, and climbed back into bed.

She came back again, the following night, and the one after. Soon, talk around the base was centered around the strict Colonel, rising star of the American Army, and his new, mysterious, red-sunglass-clad lady, who oh-so-frequently could be found entering or leaving his chambers.

Weeks passed in much this same way.

Throughout the Nineteenth Century, Morocco grew further and further into fractious political disarray. The instability in the nation, indeed, in the region, was due in large part to the insurgence and competition between the Western powers of England and France sowing unease and taking territories, one after another, for their own.

Morocco was among the last to fall and was officially placed under the protectorate of France in the year 1912, a political position under which they remained for forty-four years, until they regained their independence from France and began to live under the rule of King Mohammed V. Under the rule of the new King, many of the institutions remained, at least in name, from the regime of the French. Among these was the Direction Générale des Études, or the DGED, the Moroccan secret service charged with monitoring and enforcing Moroccan law on citizens abroad.

This is important to know because, after weeks passed much in this way for Colonel Hunter Wallace Wertheim III and the woman he called Bella Donna, the agents of the DGED, at long last, caught up to their mark.

Nadia was rudely torn from her memories by commotion from below. She had practically forgotten she was still in Brazil.

The general murmur of the crowd had changed. Something had shifted the mood from joy to what Nadia could only describe as terror. She was curious.

A woman from the crowd screamed. Then, a man.

Then, it seemed to Nadia all at once, they started running. Some toward the facilities, some away from them, but rapidly each person seemed to move at the same time.

A voice came over the speakers and urged the members of the crowd to remain calm, first in Portuguese and then in English.

Nadia saw a line of black SUVs pull up toward the side of the natatorium, and a small group of people were rushed from the doors into the cars before they sped away.

She went inside her hotel room and turned on her television.

On the news, a frightened-looking young woman spoke over the video replay of the Hungarian teenager, Devlin Gergely, seizing in the water.

Chapter 28:
Sarah Comes Home

Sarah Pulski, formerly Sarah Freeman, arrived to her home exhausted and drenched. Her trip to Brazil had resulted in a nasty cough that, even after taking antihistamines she picked up at the airport, had yet to fade.

It was already dark when she stepped out from the taxi onto the curb in front of the house that she shared with her husband.

She sighed.

Sarah Pulski's suitcase banged against the stairs as she dragged it behind her. She approached the front door and saw that the lights were not on. Bill wasn't home yet. She did not know whether to be relieved or disappointed.

The door swung open after she shoved it with the tip of her boot. It creaked as it opened. Sarah flipped on the light switch, illuminating the narrow hallway and the door to her bedroom, just to the right.

She felt something brush up against her leg.

"Oh, hey there, Seymour. You look thin, has Bill been feeding you alright?"

Her tabby cat wrapped himself around her leg and mewed up at her face. Sarah bent down to scratch him behind his ears.

"It's good to see you too, buddy."

Her cat bolted off to some dark corner of the house when she stood to continue toward her bedroom.

She brought in her suitcase and threw it on the bed before she had the chance to realize it had been stripped of the sheets. She swore under her breath. Now, not only did she have to make the bed, but the mattress was wet and dirty. She turned to go to the kitchen and find something to help her clean it. She was three full steps down the hallway before she realized what was wrong.

Slowly, Sarah Pulski looked at the walls of her hallway. The wall normally held dozens of framed photographs of her and her husband, of their wedding, their honeymoon. Tonight, there was only sun-bleached lines and nails where the paintings used to hang.

She proceeded.

Through the glass, sliding door from their kitchen to the back porch, she could see a box sitting there. When she got to it, she opened the lid.

It was a cooler. Half the ice was melted, but it kept a bottle of wine perfectly chilled, as well as some grapes, and a sandwich wrapped in butcher paper.

But when Sarah reached into the cooler, it was not for any of those things. It was for a note, sitting quite happily on top of it all.

"Bill, I know how hungry you get when you work late. Hopefully, this will help!
All yours,
-Maggie"

The *i* was dotted with a little heart.

Sarah Freeman was feeling lightheaded when she stood up. She went back inside her house, and she called her husband.

"Hey, Sarah, sweetie, I'm sorry you beat me home. I was supposed to be back hours--"

"Do you have something you want to tell me, Bill?" Sarah asked with an even tone.

There was a pause.

"Yeah...I'm sorry about the sheets, I meant to get back earlier like I was saying, but--"

"Not about the sheets, Bill."

"Not about the sheets?"

"You know what it's about," her voice was quiet, and Seymour hissed from the corner.

"Sarah, I have no idea--"

"Don't embarrass us both like that, Bill. Who is she?"

There was no sound on the other end of the line for a full minute. Sarah waited; she refused to be the one to break this silence.

"I met her through work," Bill finally said. There was no inflection in his voice.

"How long has this been going on?"

"About five months now. I'm so sorry, Sarah. I never wanted to hurt you, never wanted you to find out. I'd only ever see her when you were out of town. These last few months, it's just been so hard, you know? It just kind of happened. I'm so sorry, Sarah. I love you. I swear I do!"

It was Sarah's turn for silence. She looked around the kitchen of the house that she and her husband shared. She looked at the places on the walls where the pictures once hung. She looked at the cooler on the back porch. She did not realize how long it had been since someone had spoken out loud until…

Bill Pulski said, "Jesus Christ, Sarah, aren't you going to say something?"

Chapter 29:
Felines and Females

"Alright, Bill, calm down. Get a grip man, for fuck's sake, you're shaking."

Bill Pulski took a ragged breath and Simon Lazarus ordered two glasses of whiskey. Bill finished the first one in a single gulp. The rain had matted Bill's hair to his forehead and the two of them dripped onto the hardwood floor of Mr. Henry's bar in Cleveland, Ohio. Sun-bleached photos of Jim Brown and Bob Hope cluttered the walls. Every bar of this sort liked to litter their walls with pictures of the famous people who never stepped foot in them but maybe, just maybe, stepped foot near enough to claim their patronage as their own.

Green stained-glass lighting fixtures hung over the two billiards tables, neither of them occupied, and even though it was no longer a smoking-permitted establishment, it always seemed to Simon that Mr. Henry's had eternal clouds of cigarette smoke drifting through the air.

Bill had called Simon in a panic a little over half an hour earlier, and Simon could scarcely make out a word. Finally, Simon got a word in edgewise over Bill and told his friend to meet him at Mr. Henry's bar. It was always a little empty on Mondays.

"Okay, now tell me what happened Bill."

"Sarah got back today, Simon."

"Wasn't she supposed to?"

"Well yeah man, of course she was, but she beat me home! I was still out stuck in Moreland Hills, working that fallen bridge job by the time she was home."

"What's the problem with that? What was she expecting, a red-carpet welcome?"

Simon's half-hearted attempt at humor didn't seem to quite hit Bill's ears. Bill finished his second glass and motioned to the bartender for a third. He then began to tell the story to Simon.

Simon Lazarus listened to his best friend as Bill Pulski told him about how Sarah arrived home, about how she found the note, about how she had called, and about how he confessed to her, and now to Simon himself, how he had been seeing someone else behind her back for months.

In Mr. Henry's, Simon sat as silent as his best friend's wife had been. His veins felt like there was ice water running through them, and his stomach had sunk beneath the floorboards.

"Christ, Bill. I had no idea that you were running around on Sarah."

"Yeah, well, nobody did."

The drops from Bill Pulski's hair had finally stopped falling into his fourth glass of whiskey.

Simon stared at him, unsure of what to do. What do you do, when someone you love does something so abhorrent? Do you comfort them? Admonish them? Tell them it'll be alright? Give them a punch in the face?

Simon knew he had to at least fill the air, so he asked the only thing he could think of to ask.

"Did Sarah ever say anything back?"

Bill nodded and emptied his glass.

"She said, 'Did she like my cat?'"

Chapter 30:
The Panic Room

"What in the hell was that?"

"We're not sure we've never--"

"Never what, exactly?"

"Hey, hey, guys, take a deep breath. Ed, calm down, man."

The President of the United States and his entourage were joined in a safe house near the swimming arena by President of Brazil and his Cabinet. There was a large table in the center of the room and officers were scattered about, some standing, some sitting. Various foreign dignitaries had been brought into the room as well. Almost every single person in the room wore the same shell-shocked look on their face.

They were watching Ed Giaver and General Warthog, too distracted to notice the three mosquitoes buzzing around the room.

"Why in the hell should I calm down? Calm down?! They're the ones who put the life of the President of the United States at risk!"

The President of the United States coughed. The room went silent.

Ed Giaver stared at his president before he turned slowly, grabbed the stern-looking man by the collar with both hands, and brought him close to his own face. There was a blue vein pulsing hypnotically in Ed's temple.

"Warthog," --his voice was a menacing whisper-- "I swear to God, Warthog. Tell me you didn't read the fucking reports. Tell me you didn't read them because I need someone to punch in the fucking face right now and you sure as hell are looking like an excellent candidate. There are dozens of people out there coughing up a storm. Is there something we did not know about, Warthog?"

General Hunter Wallace Warthog III looked, for the first time since his father had passed away, like a frightened child.

"We uh, well, you see, we had the information, the thing about the files--"

"Get it out Warthog!" Ed Giaver was screaming.

"We passed on to you what we got from their Ministry of Health!"

Ivana Carvalho did not move, even when the weight of all the eyes in the room fell upon her. Her face felt cold and numb, as if all the blood had been drained from her cheeks.

She had been keeping some information to herself all day. You see, during the first four days of the Brazilian Olympic Games in 2016, the last of the Tadarida Brasiliensis, the Brazilian squat-tailed bats, with their beady yellow eyes and their blunt-tipped tails, had passed away violently. Jorge Suarez had called her, panicky and coughing with the news.

"Ivana," he said, "what do we do?"

Ivana only had one thing to say to her old friend.

She whispered it then to him as she whispered it now to this group of men and mosquitoes:

"I am very sorry, but I think you should all go home and find your families."

Chapter 31:
I-90 East

There was once a stretch of asphalt across the United States known as Interstate 90. It connected the East Coast to the West Coast through millions of tons of paved, flat rock. This was no easy feat, especially considering that, lengthwise, it stretched for 3,099 miles, from Boston, Massachusetts, to Seattle, Washington. Widthwise, it never got much wider than 36 yards, giving it roughly the proportions of a single and impossibly long thread of spider silk. It was, by far, the single longest transcontinental road in the Dwight D. Eisenhower National System of Interstate and Defense Highways. These roads were championed by President Eisenhower in the year 1956. They were long enough that, should they be picked up and lain end to end like the toys of some gargantuan toddler, they could circle the planet Earth two times over.

Simon Lazarus and his friends used to help do repairs on several roads that connected to Interstate 90, including the Innerbelt in Cleveland, just past Exit 170, located near a stretch of road known as Dead Man's Curve. It was called this on account of the fact that the way it doubled back on itself and zig-zagged around had caused the deaths of dozens of human beings on just that short stretch of asphalt.

Rather than tear up and rebuild the stretch of asphalt to make the area safer, they instead built a bar nearby and named it for the road.

Simon Lazarus was sitting in the DMC Bar with Bill Pulski and Peyton Brooks after a long day of laying asphalt. They were enjoying their third beer and each other's company, swapping stories that no one believed about their former athletic prowess while the Olympic Games played on in the background. Simon had suggested the bar as the perfect place to get Bill's mind off of Sarah.

Bill had not heard from her in four days.

This was where they were, just between one of the longest stretches of asphalt in the world and one of the deadliest, surrounded by good friends and average beer, in the city of Cleveland, Ohio, when they fell silent and watched the bar television in horror as the Hungarian teenager passed away.

At first, there was quiet.

Slowly, then, there came a low, mumbling, roar, like the first rumbling rolls of thunder on a heavy July evening, the kind that you do not really hear so much as feel, the kind that rattles your bones and permeates your entire body with a sense that something bigger is coming. One by one, the TV screens flashed a royal blue and told the viewers that the programmers were very sorry for the inconvenience and that their regularly scheduled programming would be back on shortly. By then, though, it was too late, and the people already knew something was wrong. Commotion was building. The patrons of the bar seemed to react in one of three ways: rushing out immediately, whipping out a phone and calling whomever's name was the first that popped into their minds, or ordering more booze and conversing loudly with whomever was closest to them. The noise in the bar grew for five long minutes before anyone heard more news.

Then the TV screens flashed on again, and the people were deafeningly silent. William Pulski, Peyton Brooks, and Simon Lazarus were among the many millions across the world staring intently towards the blue glow of the screen.

"The Hungarian swimmer, Devlin Gergely, has been declared dead in the water," the television reporter spoke in a clearly shaken voice.

"The cause of death, a disease of uncertain origins, has been reported in various regions throughout Brazil over the past few weeks. The virality of this disease is being investigated by the World Health Organization and the Centers for Disease Control, but it is known to locals as *Tadarida*, named after the bats that are thought to spread it.

At this time, the Olympic Village and parts of the state of Brazil have been quarantined to ensure that the disease does not spread further. Please assist and contact any local medical authorities if you see anyone exhibiting the following symptoms."

A list appeared beside the head of the news man, and it contained such phrases as 'intracerebral hemorrhaging' and 'delusional episodes' and 'death'.

Simon Lazarus's eyes glanced sidelong toward his friend, Bill Pulksi. Bill Pulski coughed into his fist.

"The President of the United States, who was in attendance at today's competition, is currently aboard Air Force One, being flown back to Washington D.C. He is planning on making an official announcement later today. Stay tuned for updates as they will be relayed to you immediately as they are brought to us."

The wave of murmurs washed back over the bar. The three friends turned to each other.

"Well, hell, it's prolly a whole lotta fuss over nuthin. Jus' like the dang ole media to whip eryone up into a stir."

But Peyton Brooks's bravado was shaky at best, and he knew Simon and Pulski could tell. None of the men wanted to say what they were feeling, so they all took a sip of beer.

Pulski took his best shot at a stoic demeanor.

"Well, and I'm sure that they're all just thirsting for the next big news story, but it definitely couldn't hurt to at least pick up some antibiotics."

"Good idea, Pulski!" Simon Lazarus quickly agreed.

"Shit, boys, all this jus reminded me a'somethin. Ya know who never takes her medications? My mama!"

Peyton Brooks shook his head, leaned back, and sighed.

"What with work here bein the way it is, I ain't had the time to see her in a month a'Sundays. I should call her on up, maybe even head down to Georgia for a spell."

"Good on you checking on your mama like that, Brooks," Simon said.

"Now that you mention it, I haven't heard from my sister in a while either."

"Well, you should swing by her place, Pulski!" Simon Lazarus encouraged. "Is Marie still out in Rossford?"

"Yeah, and she's been awful lonely since Charlie passed. All she did for twenty years was look after the senile bastard, and then he just up and croaks one day without so much as a thank you! Fuckin' rude if you ask me."

"You're not kidding."

All three took another silent sip of their beer. After a moment, Peyton Brooks spoke again.

"Ya know, I'm shore it's all just a bunch of bologna, but justa be safe..."

"Right, yeah, of course, just to be safe," said Bill Pulski.

"I mean, there can't be any harm in just checking in on them, right? At the very worst, you all get to see your family for a while, and who doesn't want that?" queried Simon Lazarus.

They agreed enthusiastically.

Peyton Brooks said he was going to get a taxi to the airport and see if he could catch the first flight to Georgia. He left fifteen dollars in cash on the bar, told the bartender to keep the change, and bid his friends farewell. Pulski coughed as he waved his hand goodbye.

"And then there were two," Simon said to Pulski. "Want to order another round?"

"Nah, better not. If I'm gonna take I-90 to Rossford, I oughta stop drinking now and head out. You staying in town?"

"Might as well. No one to visit anywhere else."

"Would you mind checking in on my place for me if I'm not back by Sunday? You know how Marie can be, I'll be painting walls till November if she has her way."

"Sure thing, Pulski."

"Thanks man, I'll see you soon."

He dropped a crumpled twenty on the counter and walked toward the door. He stopped with his hand on the door handle and turned back.

"And, uh…let me know if Sarah comes back around, will you?"

Simon gave a curt nod and watched his friend walk out the door.

Simon did not stay at the bar for much longer than that. He began to feel intensely lonely and left less than twenty minutes after Bill. He did not know that neither of his friends would reach their destinations.

Peyton Brooks's plane crashed during touchdown at the Atlanta International Airport. The pilot had a violent coughing fit upon approaching the runway and never even deployed the landing gear. There were no survivors.

Pulski was pulled over after driving erratically around Dead Man's Curve. The officer approached his vehicle expecting to find an inebriated man in the driver's seat. Instead, he found William Pulski, holding one of his teeth in his hands, retching the whole time, with the inside of his car window splattered with what looked like blood and dark, black tar.

Chapter 32:
Transcript From Presidential Address, August 8th, 2016, 16,35 EST, Location: White Sulphur Springs Bunker, WVA, via Radio and Television

[BEGIN TRANSMISSION]

[POTUS] My fellow Americans. Our Nation is a resilient one, and never one to hide from the challenges that beset us. We have been breached by pandemics before; the Yellow Fever, the Influenza, H1N1, but never have we faltered in the face of-[*indistinguishable; coughing*]. In the face of these trials. We have stood strong, and we have stood together, as we will stand-[*continued coughing*].

[ED GIAVER, off camera] Mr. President, are you-

[POTUS]Fine, Giaver, I'm fine. [*clears throat*] While in Brazil, our administration was made aware of the remarkably contagious disease, Ta...Tada...

[ED GIAVER, off camera] Tadarida, sir.

[POTUS] Thank you, Fred. Tadarida, and we have deployed not just our best doctors, but also-[*indistinguishable, coughing continues*]

[ED GIAVER, off camera] That's it, Jim, turn the cameras off, this was a bad idea. Sir, you're bleeding, we need to get you to a- SIR! Dammit, Jim, I said turn the fuckin' cameras off! The President has fallen, I repeat, POTUS down, someone get me a— —

[END TRANSMISSION]

Chapter 33:
The Minister, the Officer, and the Javali

Ivana Carvalho was dying. She knew from the first cough, from the first fever, from the moment the first of that wretched, black bile had spilled from her mouth. The delusions were coming soon, and at this point, it was only a matter of time.

She had followed her own advice, even though no one else in the Situation Room had. The Americans had gathered around their President, as if they could protect him from the bacteria already coursing through, and multiplying within, his bloodstream. The angry one, Giaver, swore at General Warthog a few more times before everyone else all rushed out into a helicopter, leaving the General behind.

General Warthog stayed there, in the room, with her for a while.

"How do we fix this?" he asked her.

"I have people looking into ways to halt the spread of the disease. They have been for quite some time, actually, but I'm not entirely sure that we can."

"There. . .there must be something we can do, isn't there?" he asked her.

Ivana said nothing but looked at him and he knew the truth, even if he refused to admit it. Which, of course, he did. He had plenty of company in his denial; he believed he would survive, that they all would survive. This singular thought was held as truth not only by the General and government of Brazil but also by most of the world, and they all continued to believe blindly in their inherent ability to survive until, one by one, they were all dead.

Ivana would be soon to join them in their death, but never in their denial.

She spent the next day orchestrating the organization of camps for the sick. With the hospitals overrun, it came to the Minister of Health to pull something together from the fractured remains of a once-proud health system.

Local police were present to help keep order. An officer approached her and asked if she was sick.

"I expect we all are, now."

Olan Oliveira's thin mustache twitched as he squinted at her. Ivana walked on, and, after a moment, he followed her. Together, they entered a tent. Officers and nurses rushed back and forth between makeshift cots, ferrying water and bedpans between them.

"There aren't enough rooms in the buildings for them all."

Ivana looked around. They were standing in the courtyard of the Olympic Village. It was barely recognizable; the newly paved track was the main transport strip. The ill populated the residential rooms that had once held athletes, although many of the rooms still did hold the ones who fell sick.

Ivana and Olan passed the pool. It had been drained of the water, and people in large coats were carrying items between them and arranging them side by side on the ground. With a sickening feeling in her gut and a sense of horror that chilled her to the bone, Nadia realized what she was seeing: a mass grave being filled. She looked away.

"Meu Deus."

"I doubt he's paying too much attention anymore, ma'am," Olan replied. His eyes were fixed on the body bags being stacked, one after another.

"Surely there's something we can do?"

"We're doing it," --a cacophony of coughs rang throughout the courtyard-- "but if you have a better idea, I'm open ears."

She nodded stiffly.

Ivana soon left the camp of Rio de Janeiro and made her way down toward the street where she lived. When she arrived there, however, she was blocked from her neighborhood by two state police officers. They told her the area was quarantined, as per orders from the Ministry of Health, no exceptions.

"But I am the *Minister* of Health."

"Sorry, ma'am, our orders are very strict," explained the first officer sternly.

"That's right," chimed in the second, "very strict."

"We just can't be letting anyone who asks us slip on by!"

"Sure can't," said the second. "No exceptions, that's what they told us, and those orders come all the way from the top."

"But I *am* the top!"

Ivana was getting frustrated.

"Well...in that case, you should know the orders, then, shouldn't you?" said the first officer slowly, like a child who just solved a particularly difficult riddle.

She gave up talking to the officers and went to return to her post in order to oversee the Brazilian Quarantine. When she arrived, however, there was the

American general in her place, barking out orders to a group of soldiers. Only some of the soldiers looked Brazilian.

"Carvalho, what are you doing here?"

The Javali was looking at her. Behind his stern eyes was something that Ivana recognized but could not name. It did not seem at home on his face.

"You tell me, General," she replied.

Her eyes and her voice were heavy.

"I have been placed in command of the Quarantine. Currently, troops are being deployed to all major airports, both public and private. We have international support pouring in, and the United Nations has granted me temporary authority over the daily operations with the BQL."

He stopped talking to look at her, and Ivana thought for a second that he was all but waiting for her to ask the obvious question. She resigned herself and asked anyway.

"BQL?"

"The Brazilian Quarantine Line, as the UN has taken to calling it."

"Right. Well, they've set up a few camps to tend to the ill. The hospitals have been overrun as of late."

"Yes, so I've heard. Is there anything else you need...Minister?" He said the last word after a pause.

She thought for a moment.

"I don't suppose you have any cigarettes, do you, General?"

Unless she was imagining things, she thought she saw the Javali stiffen.

"No, I do not. I've always hated the stuff. We'll be in touch, Minister. Thank you for stopping by."

She hesitated, wanting to say something else to the General before she left, something that he would understand, but he had already moved on, addressing a man in a dark green uniform about troop numbers or something like that. Besides, Ivana sighed to herself, he had already made it explicitly clear in the panic room that he had no intention of listening to her.

Chapter 34:
Something In Our Nature

When I was twenty-three, I drove my truck from Washington, D.C. back to my parents' home on the outskirts of Johnson City, Tennessee. In those days I tried to visit as often as I could. Even today, I do not like spending too much time away from the place that I grew up, that old country with her humble and tired mountains, so settled into the earth. Something about them almost always welcomes me with a deep sense of peace I can feel in my soul.

Almost. Not on this night.

The ride from D.C. to Johnson City is a long one, and as I crossed into Tennessee, past Bristol but not quite at Kingsport yet, the time hit one in the morning and the sky opened up and a storm began unlike any I had ever seen or any I have ever seen since. I could scarcely see through my windshield and my headlights illuminated only rain. I was only a few dozen miles from home, though, so I pressed on.

I came down the hill, approaching my old house. It was just after two and the rain was battering the roof of my car. I could not hear the radio, but I was almost home; I just wanted to get there. I sped up.

Lightning split the sky, and I could see the road. Or rather, what was left of it.

Asphalt had washed away, leaving a gash of crumbled earth. There was a bang followed with deafening grinding. The truck's axle was snapped before I even reached the other side.

As I careened off the side of the road, I thought to myself:

What a ridiculous way to die.

When I look back at that moment, I still am surprised that I was more concerned about the manner of my death than I was that I was about to die. There must be something in our nature that feels no fear of death, or else I would have felt it there.

When I pulled my head off the steering wheel, the hood of the truck was crumpled in on itself and smoking, even in the rain. Another bolt of lightning illuminated the world. My truck was resting against the split and splintered trunk of the bitternut hickory tree. A light flickered on in my parents' home.

The next morning, the rain had ended and the sky was clear and my truck was no longer smoking, but the tree was still shattered and split right down the middle. That morning, although I was never quite sure why, I called the girl I had met at that tree so many years earlier for the first time in a long time. The next day, we went to get coffee and talked for hours.

And we never really stopped.

Well. Not until now, I suppose.

Chapter 35:
The General and the Jewel Thief

The last American General to ever be stationed in Brazil wandered through the camp that once was the Olympic Village. In what could only be described as a truly loathsome display, most of his soldiers had abandoned their posts in an attempt to "get medical attention" or "find their families," but in his soul, Warthog knew these were just the most popular excuses that day for being a simple goddamned coward.

So, with what was unknown to him as his last truly lucid day on earth, he proceeded down to the medical camp to see if he could find any of his soldiers, or at the very least, conscript some new ones.

What he found astounded him, or rather, it would have, if he had the capacity to still be astounded.

Rows after rows of cots were filled with dying men. The sick women, with their children, were a few tents over.

Before the General lay acres of lurking death, and he stared at the inevitable, and he felt suddenly and profoundly aware. He could hear every cough and smell the sweet stench of death.

The chorus of coughing drowned out any thoughts he might have had when he arrived about recruiting more soldiers.

And so, between the cots, the General walked in silence, meeting the eyes of every man who looked his way, but they never seemed to really see him. Often, when they did, they would call him by a name foreign to him as if they were recognizing not him, but rather the concept of a human before them.

Without noticing, he found himself in the women's tent. He was not entirely sure where he had crossed over; the broken eyes still all looked the same to him. His pace did not slow. It did not gain speed. He walked without thinking, and walked only to continue seeing those eyes.

Ahead, he saw a familiar figure. That cop that had kept bothering him, Olivia. No, that wasn't it. Whatever it may be, his name hardly mattered; he was crouching at the foot of a bed, speaking softly to its occupant, an elegant woman, with only one eye.

The General approached the cot and every footstep felt like a mile. The Officer said something that Hunter did not hear. He could not hear anything, save for the thunderous pumping of his own heart and the echo of a name he once knew, a name he had whispered lovingly, years ago, late at night, on the Israeli coast.

Bella Donna?

Had he been standing there for hours? The Officer was staring at him, and he appeared to still be talking. More importantly, she was looking at him now too, and, in the one good eye, a flit of recognition behind the clouds that Tadarida had left in her mind.

"Hunter?"

Her voice was barely a whisper, but it was the first thing to break through the waves of memory he was sinking into, unable to tell what truly was now and what was then. He was in the Mediterranean heat as he stared at her in Brazil.

The only sound he could make was a croak, as close of an approximation as he could make to the name he knew she held.

"Nadia?"

Her rattling chuckle turned quickly to a cough.

"I liked it better when I was Bella."

He could not reply, so she continued.

"Is this really you? I have seen you so many times. Olan, is there a man here?" She looked up to the

Officer. The Officer nodded, his face pale behind his pencil-thin mustache.

"I don't care if you are real or not, Hunter. I'm sorry. I'm so sorry."

Still, he could not speak.

"I lied to you. I could not trust anyone, and by the time I could, I was too far deep in the lie and…"

"Why didn't you find me?"

The General was as surprised as anyone to hear his own voice break free of the spell he was held in.

"I should have, Hunter." Her one good eye was glinting.

Could it actually be a tear? He had never seen her with a tear in her eye. He watched as it traced her face. He was tracing her face, decades ago, following the same path that the tear was taking. She was lying on his chest. She was lying in the cot. She was whispering.

"I love you, Hunter."

"What?" he gasped.

Clarity. It was the only thing she could have said to bring clarity. He was certain where he was. He was in the tent in the Olympic Village in Brazil, and she was lying there, broken body and broken spirit, but her voice remained unbroken.

"I love you." Her tears began to flow freely, finally unimpeded.

Hunter backed away, slowly at first, then with greater speed. Out of the tent, out of the Village, back to his lonely, sparse apartment, he ran leaving his love and, eventually, his sanity behind him.

General Hunter Wallace Wertheim III pulled from his bedside drawer the only personal possession he valued: a small, golden cross on a thin chain.

And alone, the General began to cry.

In the Olympic Village, Nadia Lehcar Bin-Said slipped in and out of reality, with her friend Officer Olan Oliviera by her side. Her screams and her retches were intermixed, and Olan did not know which broke his heart worse.

She was dead before the sun broke the morning.

The Officer stared at his dead friend for hours that day, and the General held tight to his cross.

Chapter 36:
Freeman

I suppose I ought to tell what became of Sarah Freeman, formerly Sarah Pulski, after she hung up on her husband.

It only took four days for the news stations to start reporting on a mysterious disease spreading throughout the area, and only four more before the news anchors were too ill to do the reporting.

Sarah Freeman, formerly Sarah Pulski, during all this time was alone in her home. Seymour kept her company at first, but before long she was too delirious to know to feed him, and by the time she had realized his absence, he had been gone for three days.

She needn't have worried, however, as house cats are particularly adept at surviving on their own.

Human beings, as it would turn out, are not.

Chapter 37:
The Last Patrol

Officer Olan Oliveira wandered through the rain in what remained of the Olympic Village. He walked alone, except, of course, for all the people.

On the large part, though, they were almost all dead, so I suppose they did not quite count.

Olan's shirt was torn at the sleeve. The only possessions that he still held were his badge and a beautiful diamond necklace that an American tourist refused to negotiate over.

What a silly woman she was.

He drifted out of the women's tent and down towards the track. It was cluttered, with sheets and bandages clinging limply to the damp ground. They fluttered as he passed by. Through the fog in the air, and in his mind, he was vaguely aware that this was the same track that he had seen runners on just days earlier, preparing for their races. The same buildings that had housed those demigods now stretched toward the heavens, filled with the dead and those soon to join them, and the Village that had once beat like the heart of some great beast seemed to be growing stiller by the moment.

There was coughing and crying echoing from all directions. It seemed to Olan, though, that they were simply the noise of a stiff breeze. He walked on.

Olan passed the mass grave that had once been the pool and, as he did, stuck his hands in his pockets. There was something there, but he could not recall what it could be.

Out of his pocket, he pulled a stack of cash: Brazilian reals, US dollars, euros, pounds, yen. They were what was left of the gifts and donations from many concerned tourists he had run into. At the time, it was quite heartwarming how passionate they were about donating to the force; often he was so moved by their generosity that he fast-tracked whatever they were concerned about. That cash must have been sitting in his pockets for days, weeks.

There comes a time after the death of hope in some lives that is difficult to describe. After the fall of that time where there seems to still be a chance, a thing worth fighting for. After not only the flames but the embers, too, have grown cold, but while there is still life in the body. In 1967, at the University of Pennsylvania, Martin Seligman performed an experiment on a group of dogs. He put them in cages with wired floors and ran currents through the metal ground, shocking them with hundreds of volts. There was an obstacle in their way, and on the other side the floor was not wired. He found that, no matter how impedimental the obstacle, so long as they could pass it to safety, they would.

So he wired the other part of the floors.

After a while, to the number, each and every dog would curl up in a corner of their cage as the electric shock pulsed through their body, just waiting for it to stop.

And so Officer Olan Oliveira walked on through the mist on his last patrol, and behind him, like leaves in the wind, blew the currency of a dozen countries.

Chapter 38:
Burning

"Albi? Albi, are you in here?"

The door wouldn't budge. Ivana put her shoulder into the wood and finally it opened a crack. Smoke trickled out from the small opening. It took a few more shoves for the door to be properly open.

"Albi?"

The room Ivana stepped into was dark; thick and tattered shades were drawn across the windows. Empty takeout containers, cigarette packets, and liquor bottles littered the hardwood floor to the point that Ivana could barely see it. There was a flurry of motion.

"Albi? Is that you?"

There was muttering. In the corner of the room, there was a single, stark white lamp, silhouetting what Ivana could only think was a wall. As she moved forward, she realized she was staring at a massive canvas, impossibly large for the diminutive artist who was working on it. A cloud of smoke clung to the ceiling above the light, as if the Angel of Death were patiently observing the scene.

As she approached the light, she could make out Albi de Foix's tiny legs scurrying back and forth, from one side of the canvas to the other, as he talked to himself all the while.

"The world is burning, Albi, what are you doing?"

"What was that? Who's there?" the raspy voice demanded.

He brandished his paint brush like a saber in Ivana's direction.

"It's me, Fox! Put that thing down, don't you know what's going on?"

"What's going on, Ivana, is that I have finally begun my masterpiece!"

He came out from behind the canvas, knocking over a candle in the process. Ivana rushed to stomp it out.

"Albi, that's great and all but we need to--"

"No, Ivana. I don't think you understand. I have begun. This is my life, on this canvas. My masterpiece has been started, and now I must fin--"

His sentence was interrupted by his own retching.

"The city is on fire out there Albi, we can't stay here!"

Albi de Foix's eyes lit up. He stumbled towards the window and tore open the blinds. They both squinted at the new light streaming into the room.

"On fire, you say." His voice was but a whisper. "Yes…yes, I think I have room for that."

"What does that mean, Albi?"

He was already piling his paint and brushes into a small bag and taking the canvas from its stand, carrying it as best he could. He shoved past Ivana and took off down the stairs and off onto the road, leaving her standing along in the room.

She looked around his apartment and knew that when she shut the door, there would be no one again to open it.

So Ivana left and she walked until she found herself at the house of God, but the doors were locked. She sat down in the parking lot, where she would remain as the rest of the world crumbled and collapsed around her. She prayed, occasionally. She prayed for rest. She prayed for health, but most of all, she prayed for answers.

She would receive none.

Chapter 39:
Strange Thunder

I moved to the city when I was still a young man, before my wife was my wife, but after I finally had gathered the good sense to ask her to change that fact. I had taken my first job as a writer and moved into a small flat by myself. It was a bare place; a mattress on the floor and a folding table I used as a desk. There was barely enough space for an ashtray.

In your head, or rather, in mine, you can imagine a city in all kinds of weather. I could see it in the rain, in the snow, with lightning flashing through the sky. All of it.

All of it, that is, except for the thunder.

Perhaps it was foolish of me. I know it was. Still, I was startled that first night, when the storm rolled in off the sea, and the thunder rattled the windows of the apartment complexes that stretched so high into the sky that it seemed to me that they must be the ones pulling the thunder itself from those clouds. I thought, at first, that there had been a car crash outside my building. I was looking outside my window to find the source of the noise when another bolt of lightning streaked through the sky and the thunder cracked loud again in its wake.

It was as though I had heard thunder for the first time in my life.

I sat back down and listened as the rain began to splatter against my window. The rain smelled different in the city. It reminded me almost of copper, but the thunder sounded all the same.

I thought of the woman who would become my wife. My apartment seemed extraordinarily empty to me in that moment, as this strange thunder rolled through the towering concrete of the strange city. I called her, but the she didn't pick up.

"Hey babe. Did you know that in the city the thunder…well, never mind. I miss you darling. I'll see you soon."

I shut off the phone and looked out of the window. Out at the rain.

I should have brought her with me. She wanted to go, but I insisted that she stayed behind. I'd come back for her, and I didn't want her living a life like this.

Most of my days were composed of me waiting in offices and for phone calls and in line at agencies, doing everything I could to get my first book published. Then, I would go home, write some more, and go to bed alone, missing her. All those days passed in much that way; they passed me by while I was waiting for better days to happen, expecting that one day they just would, but in truth, those were simply the bulk of the days.

They're silly, aren't they, the things you think are important when you're young? I did not want her living a 'life like that,' whatever that meant. It would have been a life together. She knew that. I didn't, and I didn't listen.

She always was smarter than me.

Chapter 40:
A Masterpiece; Life on Canvas

Albi stood at the top of Corcovado, with the outstretched arms of a God he never believed in to his back. The trek up the mountain was a difficult one, but I suppose anything is possible with a determined spirit and a disease-addled mind so far gone from comprehending your own mortal, physical limits that the thought of stopping never once enters it.

And so Albi de Foix climbed the 223 steps to the top of the mountain and looked out over his city with brush in hand.

The vantage from that point was breathtaking. Albi could see the entirety of the harbor, and Ivana was right; the city was burning.

Plumes of smoke rose from buildings, from the Barra da Tijuca all the way to the Museum of Tomorrow. The rain had let up, and the sun was setting on Brazil, cracking through the clouds on the horizon with beams of light filtered through the rising smoke, and the whole city looked as if it were ablaze.

Albi was feverishly giggling as his brush flew from side to side on the canvas. It only stopped when he broke into fits of coughing, which, as it happened, occurred more and more frequently.

The sun glinted closer to the horizon and the smoke began to turn red. Albi stood back from his canvas and gazed upon it with tears in his eyes, gently resting his hand on the cloth.

"Done. I'm--"

Albi de Foix's final bit of coughing overtook him. He sank to his knees and, in doing so, dragged his fingers across the face of the painting. With panic in his eyes, Albi de Foix retched and choked, bile and blood mixing indistinguishably on his face as he finally fell still, lifeless.

The final work from, perhaps, the last great artist in human history would stand on this mountain until the end of man, a few days later. Not a single person would live to see the final masterpiece ever painted.

If they had, they would have seen a giant canvas, largely blank, save for a few splotches of red, dancing across the lower half, looking almost like flames. Upon closer inspection, these imaginary viewers would have realized, to their hypothetical horror, that there was no

paint used in the entirety of work; there was only
blood, drawn across the canvas in short, sporadic
strokes.

There was no paint. There was only life, and, in the
end, the absence of it.

Chapter 41:
The BQL (Brazilian Quarantine Line)

Tadarida spread rapidly and wildly. Within hours of the internationally broadcasted deaths of Devlin Gergely and the President of the United States, the governments of the world came together in an attempt to quarantine much of eastern Brazil. This did not work quite as well as they had planned.

The international community inside of Brazil at this point was massive, wealthy, and restless. They wanted out. They wanted to go home, and, like most diseases, they wanted to spread. At first, they did not take the plague entirely seriously. No one had yet grasped the magnitude and the reach it could have, nor did anyone, aside from Jorge Suarez, Ivana Carvalho, and their team, fully understand just how quickly it could be transmitted. All they knew was how badly they wanted to leave.

General Hunter Wallace Warthog III had been placed in charge of the operations of the BQL, but he had increasing difficulty enforcing them. His men were either deserting or deceasing by the dozens.

Between coughing fits, General Warthog would receive reports and pass out demands, trying to keep up morale. He believed they would succeed and see through to the other side of this struggle, exhausted and diminished but victorious nonetheless.

After two weeks, the borders were so insufficiently manned that he was forced to report to the Minister of Health that the quarantine would not hold.

The fall of the Brazilian Quarantine was the end of the last great hope for mankind.

It had held for just over two weeks.

Governments around the world had either prepared for the worst, ignored the problem in the hopes the disease would run its course and be cured, or collapsed altogether, which was really the most sensible option.

General Warthog would remain in Brazil, however. Hunter Wallace Warthog III was a proud military man, raised by proud military men, and he'd be damned if he was going to leave his post just because the situation looked a little rough.

Besides, he would not have been able to leave, even if he wanted to. He hadn't the slightest idea where he was anymore and was coughing far too much to ask.

Chapter 42:
Alive and Well

The Brazilian Quarantine Line stood for a total of seventeen days. Planes were grounded (except for the rich) and experimental medicines were distributed (except for the poor), but nothing seemed to work. Without any substantial progress made in fighting the disease, and party leaders becoming sick and passing away, the Brazilian government was forced to acknowledge their failure to prevent the spread of Tadarida. This was made official when it was reported to the Minister of Health from the General in command of maintaining the quarantine that they had finally given up all hope.

There were skirmishes breaking out all over the world, but nothing was to be permanent. Likewise, aid and assistance efforts were started and halted on a local and global scale in a matter of days.

No less than three terrorist organizations claimed credit for the plague, but were all quickly wiped out themselves.

The Americas were the first to go. The virility of Tadarida was unprecedented. The mortality rate among those afflicted reached nearly 100 percent. Those that 'survived' the initial symptoms of the sickness were left in a permanent mental state of delusion and most of them perished by means of accidental suicide or starvation.

Europe followed soon thereafter; many of the tourists that had gone home before the death of the Hungarian swimmer had spread the disease to their relatives, neighbors, and coworkers. Everywhere, Tadarida was spreading, and it was impossible to stop.

Mankind was ending, and quickly.

Of course, it is important to think of everything with some sense of perspective and acknowledgment of context. For example, life on Earth, generally speaking, was about to enter a period of renaissance and growth unlike anything seen since the Cambrian explosion. Flora and fauna worldwide would use this opportunity to retake the vast expanses of global surface area mankind had attempted to tame, and they would be able to undo centuries of ecological damage that human scientists had long since speculated, incorrectly, may be irreversible.

In addition, the global temperature would stabilize, risk of Nuclear Armageddon would drop dramatically, and many species on the brink of extinction would make a remarkable comeback, including the African black rhino and the Brazilian flat-headed tree toad.

All wars and conflicts would be solved, albeit in a very Gordian knot sort of way. The Great Barrier Reef would never quite return to its zenith, but the surrounding ecosystem would eventually begin to flourish once more, in a way it had not in nearly three hundred years. The great forests of the world, from the redwood forest in North America to the rain forest in South, began reclaiming their respective continents, and, after just a few decades, even the stars would begin to shine nearly as clearly and brightly and truly across the night sky as they once had, years and years before.

Although the idea of a Planet Earth that resembles this image may cause you to shudder in terror, fear not for our world. As I have mentioned, the world of Simon Lazarus is very much a fictional one, and you can rest assured that mankind is alive and well in ours to this very day, and you and I will never be subject to the terror that would be the pure, uninterrupted view of the night sky at any point throughout our lives.

Chapter 43:
Storms at Sea

In all, 2.9 billion human beings had been watching the Olympic Games when Devlin Gergely passed away. This was a television-broadcasting record, both for the most watched event of all time as well as the best publicized death, and one that would stand until the last man on earth would die. This fact, which would normally be a mark of pride for network executives worldwide, was somewhat tarnished by the brevity of the amount of time within which they were able to enjoy it, as that last death would occur a mere forty-one days later.

The Cleveland Hopkins International Airport was swarming with people. Simon Lazarus had come to catch a flight, but upon arriving, realized he had nowhere to go, and so he entered a bar inside the airport and sat down to order a drink.

The place was small and dark and looked exactly like all other airport bars, with generic neon lights, shelves of backlit liquor, and bottles on the top that were covered with a layer of dust.

"Jack and Coke, please," Simon said to the bartender.

The TV in the background showed a news anchor, detailing through a muted screen the fall of the Brazilian Quarantine. He looked nervous.

"You coming or going?" asked the bartender.

"Neither, actually," Simon replied. He looked away from the television and sipped his dark drink. He let the light burn linger for a while before he took a second drink. "Are you trying to skip town? You know, get yourself out of here while you can?"

The bartender paused for a beat. He replied to Simon with a question of his own. "Have you ever been in the Navy? Or worked on a ship?"

Simon shook his head. He was paying much closer attention to the bartender now. He had dark skin with lines that looked tanned into his face and a gray stubble that fought its way through the tough-looking leather of his cheeks to give his chin a texture roughly that of sandpaper. The bartender nodded and continued.

"I was in the U.S. Navy for seven years. We were on the Pacific, working a standard deployment, when, off the starboard side, we saw a storm coming towards us. It moved slowly, but it stretched so long to each end of the horizon that it seemed to us like it was the only thing in the entire world. Have you ever seen a storm at sea?"

Again, Simon shook his head no.

"No," said the bartender, "no, I'm not leaving town."

Simon stopped talking to the bartender after that. He paid for his whiskey and got up and left.

While he was walking out of the airport, Simon Lazarus fell to his knees and began to cough.

Chapter 44:
Damn Birds

I peered out the window, across the bar from where I sat, and squinted; I was unused to the sunshine. There was a seagull sitting there, staring at me.

All of a sudden, a memory resurfaced, one that I had not thought of in a long, long time. It was of a conversation I had once had with my wife, before she was my wife, before we had ever kissed, but long after I had fallen in love with her. We were still young and innocent and both full of life, not yet fourteen years of age. We were sitting in a classroom, in the back, where those adolescent youths with a gleam in their eyes, the ones who aim to misbehave, all too often choose to sit, naïvely believing themselves to be invisible from four rows back.

In our stiff Catholic school seats, we sat there among our peers chanting the Lord's Prayer in mindless Latin, and I was just happy to be near her.

"Pater Noster, qui est en Caelis, sanctificum nomen tuum."

She had leaned over to whisper to me, quite unprovoked, sending my star-crossed heart into a flurry.

She told me, "When I die, Peter, when I die, I am going to be reincarnated as a bird, and I am going to fly around by the ocean forever."

We were young and stupid. In the back of that classroom, we cawed like crows and flapped our arms like wings and rolled into laughter as the rest of the class stared on in utter confusion. Eventually, the teacher had to demand that we leave so that she might have the smallest chance to regain the order in her room.

A thought occurred to me for the first time now, just now, as I stared at this gray gull, and as it stared right back at me; as delusional as it was, and as absurd as it sounded, there was absolutely nothing I could do or think of to prove that young girl wrong.

I watched the bird, and it watched me, until it cawed and flew away.

I ordered another drink. It was only a bird, after all, I told myself. Just another damn bird. It's not her.

She's gone.

If you love someone so deeply, so truly, you give a piece of yourself to them, and then they choose to leave, where does that piece of you go? Is there more of you in the world now, or is there less?

Chapter 45:
What Did the Bartender Put in My Drink?

I wanted a whiskey but this tastes like gin.

Chapter 46:
Ivana, Again

Fuck it. I don't really care about what she's up to, honestly.

Chapter 47:
General Warthog the Last

General Hunter Wallace Warthog the Last died of the disease Tadarida exactly twenty-two days after Devlin Gergely. Although, if such a record could have been kept, Tadarida would not have been his official cause of death. Technically, he was killed when his body struck the ground after a fall from a ten-story window. His last words, promptly before hitting the ground, were:

"I think I forgot my wallet!"

His second to last words were:

"I'm going out for cigarettes, don't wait up."

Chapter 48:
Advice

"Do you think that is a satisfying enough end for the General?"

"Mm?"

"The Javali. Are you sure that's the end you want for him?"

"I thought it was keeping in pace with his character. Why, what did you think?"

"I don't know. I thought he kind of, deserved more. This whole, almost, tragic backstory, just to end like that? I liked the General."

"So did I."

"He's one of my favorite characters. His death though, I'm not sure. Maybe it could use more detail, you know? Ivana's death, that scene had so much true emotion behind it. The General's just seems, impersonal, I guess. Distant. Now, I know that he's your character--"

"He's not mine; I'm just telling his story."

"…Well then, tell his story in a way he could be proud to have it be told."

Chapter 49:
General Warthog the Last:
Revisited

Diseases often kill you by infecting your body and breaking it down over time. The especially deadly diseases have a tendency to chip, chip, chip away at all your remaining years, until there is no more time left for you to live. A rarer, select group of ailments may even attack your mind, deteriorating it a little bit at a time until you can no longer even fathom the tomorrow that would not come.

Tadarida was not like these diseases.

By the time General Warthog realized this, however, it was too late for him to even begin to explain it.

The visible symptoms began by deteriorating his body, and before long he held several of his teeth in his hands, but the way it stole years was different. The years the disease was taking from General Hunter Wallace Warthog III were not the years from the end of his life; they were the years from the beginning.

His life was fading behind him as quickly as his future rushed to its close. His years were as though he had never lived them, and with every hour that passed, his life was that much more less lived. It was erasing him, and before long, not only would he no longer be, but General Hunter Wallace Wertheim III would have never even been.

His memory was flying, taking him backward through time, as the days of his life disappeared from his mind.

He was in Israel, ordered to court-martial the only woman he would ever love, her true name revealed to him at last, and her betrayal on his lips like her last kiss, like poison, like Bella Donna.

"Nadia," he had whispered as he walked into her empty cell surrounded by the Moroccan secret service.

Nearly empty. There was only a small gold cross where his lover had been.

And then, she was gone.

He was receiving the call that his father had died. He was asked to speak at the funeral, but he was on deployment, and as the old man always said, duty comes first.

And then the funeral he never went to and the grave he never visited were gone.

His father had called him "Tripp" when he was younger. Short for "the Third".

How he hated that nickname.

"Tripp!" he'd call. "Get over here boy."

These calls to action were almost invariably followed by some sort of anger from the old man. Tripp's bed wasn't made, or the floor wasn't cleaned, or he had received a less-than-satisfactory mark in school.

On this day in particular, his father had gotten a call from school. The Third had been caught in a brawl in the school yard.

"Did he win?" Was his father's only question.

He did not, and now here he was, in the basement, being taught firsthand the benefits of a strong right hook.

"Protect your chin, Tripp! Keep that left hand up, I won't be able to get your face again like last time if you just, hell, listen up!" the old man yelled, through puffs of a cigarette.

And then this failure was gone.

He was a child. It was one of the only memories he had of his mother. It was so old, he didn't even know that the memory was still there, or if it had ever even happened at all, but there she sat, both of their hands wrapped around a worn-down blue crayon.

She was teaching him to spell his name.

"Now an *n*...good, yeah, just like that! You're going to be so smart, aren't you, Hunter?"

Her voice was as light as the sunshine streaming through the open window. He looked up at his mother and smiled.

And then General Hunter Wallace Wertheim III was gone.

Chapter 50:
Stamp of Approval

"Better?"

"Yeah, yeah that's loads better. That's the death he deserves, which is really all any of us can ask for, isn't it?"

Chapter 51:
St. Margaret's

Business was booming for St. Margaret's Hospital of Cleveland, Ohio, in the days and weeks following the Olympic Games and the unprecedented spread of Tadarida. They were filled to capacity over at St. Margaret's and the board was thrilled. They had been growing concerned over the finances of the hospital for the last few months, but now, with the demand for treatment going way up and showing no signs of slowing, there was no reason at all to be concerned about cash flow any longer.

Of course, a nasty side effect of the increase in demand was that the people of Cleveland were dying by the score. Although this was upsetting to even the most stoic of doctors, they all had to admit, it was certainly good for business.

When Simon Lazarus was checked in to St. Margaret's, they placed a bright yellow bracelet on his wrist. The plan had been, originally, to establish a quarantine ward inside the hospital. This had worked for a time, but, as more and more infected patients arrived, almost the entirety of St. Margaret's began to be dedicated to treating the disease. Before long, there was almost no room in the hospital for anyone else. Though the word was only seldom used, everyone at the hospital understood that this was a fully-fledged epidemic, and the odds of preventing the spread were looking grimmer by the day.

Simon's gums were black and he had a cough, but he had out lived his last three roommates, so that was cause for optimism. He knew he was getting no worse because the pattern was clear by now. On the other side of the gray curtain, they would wheel in a new gurney. There would be coughing at first, deep and loud and punching, more a bark than anything. That would be shortly followed by the retching.

Oh, God, how he hated the retching. They could never breathe while they were retching, and their shuddering gasps made Simon shudder as well. The retching was followed inevitably by delusions. Sometimes, they saw an old lover; sometimes, their best friend. Seldom, they saw Simon. Always, they saw God. Then, it would be over. A new gurney would be wheeled in, and the curtain would begin to cough once more.

Simon did not want to watch as they pulled a sheet over the bed to his left, so he turned away to look toward the window.

Outside the hospital, down on the street, Simon saw a man burst out from the front doors. He ran out into the parking lot in his gown, his bare ass visible as the cloth flapped around him. On his wrist was the bright yellow armband of a Tadarida patient, and he appeared to be holding a can of some sort. Behind him, running at full speed, were two security guards. The man was screaming something that Simon could not hear, and the guards pulled out their guns. The man swung the object he was holding toward his feet, and the trim of his gown burst into flames.

The fire spread rapidly, engulfing his entire body. He collapsed to the ground, screaming and writhing in pain until the guards emptied eleven shots into his body.

He lay still, then, the flames still licking up and surrounding the corpse. Dark, black smoke billowed into the sky. The guards walked back inside.

"Why do you think they shot him, when he was trying to kill himself anyway?" Simon asked the room at large.

He looked around, and suddenly realized that he was all alone.

Simon looked back out the window, and he watched as the fire burned and the guards walked back towards the hospital and another ambulance pulled up filled with new patients needing treatment.

They were in luck; a bed had just opened up.

Chapter 52:
Hell

My father was born in Hell, back when it was still just a small town in midwestern Pennsylvania.

The landfill of Centralia, Pennsylvania, was filled to the brim by the time I was five years old. The town did not know what to do with all the waste, so they did the only thing they could think of.

They burned it.

There was a problem with this plan, though. The landfill the town had been using for years was nothing more than a repurposed coal mine. Within days, fire was raging through the tunnels underneath the town. Roads were cracking as the ground crumbled beneath homes, and flames licked higher and higher toward the sky through shattered earth.

I was five years old when the fire started, and we stayed for another five as my father tried to help put it out.

Eventually, the flames rose too high, and we left Hell behind us as we moved South to Tennessee.

Chapter 53:
Fair Trades and Bird Nests

The fire in the parking lot had gone out. Up in Simon's room, the nurses wheeled in a new gurney.

"This room just opened up, we can put him in here."

"William? Can you hear me?"

Simon's last roommate coughed hard in response.

"Okay, good. We're going to set you up here, and we'll be right back, alright?"

Another coughing fit of affirmation. The nurses left the room. Simon's newest roommate stopped coughing and took a long, rattling inhalation. His breathing was shallow. Simon looked again out the window by his bed and wondered with a mild curiosity why he was feeling no worse than when he checked in.

There was a bird's nest on the windowsill. It was not large, but it was remarkably intricate, the type of nest a mother bird must have spent days on, constructing it out of leaves and stray paper and perfectly selected twigs and she ought to have been very proud of the thing, but the nest was empty, not even a single egg.

Simon had been studying the nest for the last two days and had concluded that the bird family had simply forgotten about it and left the nest there to stay, where it would remain, presumably, until some large storm came and wiped it away forever. Simon tried to decide whether or not this made him sad, but reached no definitive conclusion either way.

His roommate was coughing again.

An hour later, the nurses returned with an IV for his roommate and a puzzled look for Simon. They were still certain the disease would get him eventually, but for now, they were simply surprised at his resilience.

The retching had begun, and Simon tried to ignore it. The sunlight was streaming in through the immaculate window. It was kind of a beautiful day.

"And I, thank, because you can, don't call me, go to hell, dammit, GO TO HELL! Simon, where's Simon?"

The curtain was speaking through sobs in a voice that was familiar to Simon Lazarus. It couldn't be. . . God, please do not let it be.

"...Pulski?"

"THAT. IS. NOT. MY. NAME!"

The curtain's sob turned into a cough turned into retching, such terrible, terrible retching unlike what Simon had heard before. He thought the curtain may never breathe again, but at last it gasped.

The sobs returned.

Simon leaped from the bed and ripped the curtain aside. Lying there were the skin and bones of William Pulski, and not much else, not even most of the memories his head had once held. The years had been quietly slipping out of his mind, one after another, leaving only the vaguest of impressions that something might be missing, not that he could venture a guess as to what it might be, but Simon thought he saw a look of recognition in his best friend's eyes.

"Bill? Wha-? I, I thought you left town, Bill, I-"

"Simon. I want Simon."

"Bill, I'm here I,-"

"His name. I'm not his name. I'm not- I'm not him!" One of the strongest men Simon had ever known was lying here in this bed, broken.

"Bill."

Bill had begun retching again. Simon tried not to ignore it. He got a pan for the bile spilling from his friend's mouth. Several teeth fell out. There was blood there, too.

Bill was struggling to breathe. He sucked in but got no air. His body convulsed and his arms spasmed. Simon ran into the hallway.

"Nurse! Nurse! Help! Help my friend! Please, PLEASE!"

A man in blue scrubs rushed into the room but the delusional ranting had stopped. The retching had stopped. The coughing had stopped. Everything had stopped.

William Pulski was declared dead in Cleveland, Ohio at 4:37 PM on September 5th, 2016. It was kind of a beautiful day.

Simon Lazarus sat and stared at the empty bed on the other side of the curtain, and he held back tears. You see, a long time ago it was decided that it made everyone uncomfortable when grown men divulged their feelings, so the world silently agreed that instead of feelings, men got to have beer.

It no longer seemed like a fair trade.

Chapter 54:
After

After my wife's funeral, I sat at a bar with my best friend, Bill Pulski, whose name I gave to the best friend of Simon Lazarus. I told Bill I had begun a novel, years ago, with a character that I named after him. I said I had never finished it, but I was thinking about picking it up again, and did he mind that there was a character that bore his likeness that might make his way into a work of my fiction. He told me to go right ahead. I don't think he quite believed me at the time that such a work would ever be out there. Truth be told, I was not so sure myself.

We sat there for a long time after that, not saying much. When you've been friends for so long, sometimes there isn't much left to say. You know it all already, and, maybe most importantly, you know when to say nothing at all. So, we sipped on our drinks, and Bill waited for me to talk.

A few years ago, Bill's father had passed away, and I remembered how I had once sat with Bill in very much the same way he sat there with me. I asked him how he got through it and how he managed to keep going with that pain.

Bill said to me, "Often, often I am reminded of that old saying; sometimes, things have to get worse."

"Before they get better?" I asked, after a heavy pause.

"What was that?" Bill replied.

"Before they get better? Isn't that how the saying goes? You know, things have to get worse, before they get better?"

He laughed and shook his head.

"Before they get better," Bill mused, rolling the phrase around in his mouth to see how it felt there.

He shook his head and raised his glass to his mouth.

"You're not pulling my leg, are you? Damn, what will they think of next?"

Chapter 55:
Stars

Today we know that stars are flaming balls of gas, unfathomable in size, unfathomable in temperature, burning at an unfathomable distance away. Although, we know this now, human beings only came to acquire this knowledge very recently. In fact, centuries ago, the ancient Greeks believed that the stars were the souls of heroes of old, placed above us in the sky by the gods to tell us the beautiful, tragic stories of those who left us with only a shimmering shadow of who they might have been.

Of course, we know better now. Still though, for all that we've learned over those centuries, it seems to me that the stars don't shine nearly as brightly as they did when they were heroes.

Ralph Waldo Emerson once wrote:

If the stars should appear one night in a thousand years, how would men believe and adore; and preserve for many generations the remembrance of the city of God which had been shown! But every night come out these envoys of beauty, and light the universe with their admonishing smile.

I've always liked that quote, and for the longest time, like many armchair philosophers, I would invoke it late at dinner parties, lamenting the state of the modern man and his forsaking of the wonders of the natural world.

I no longer feel connected to this sentiment, though, not as I once did.

If the stars should appear but once in a thousand years, I wish I could have taken her up to the highest spot in the darkest country. I wish we could have sat there, all by ourselves. I wish I could have had the chance to never see the stars, to never look up for the first time as they shone and sparkled and twinkled in a far-too-often dark night sky. I wish I could have watched her face as she saw them for the first time.

I wish a lot of things these days, but now this is what I wish for most from God and Ralph Waldo Emerson:

I wish for that one night.

Just. One. Night.

Chapter 56:
Before

Simon Lazarus's father died by the time Simon was six years old. Not that Simon would ever know that. He had never met his father.

His father, who was named Inacio, died from complications from the disease gonorrhea, which was, in fact, highly treatable. He contracted it in the back seat of a taxicab in the port city of Buenos Aires, Argentina from a prostitute named Castizia. He was thirty-four years old when he died, and he never knew he had a son.

Before he died, he was brought to Hospital Sirio-Libanes in São Paulo, where he had collapsed. While he was there, he was treated by Dr. Ivana Carvalho, a young, up-and-coming physician, before she had begun to be respected nationally for her work in infectious diseases. His delirious mind, which had already lost most of its functions and was only a few hours from giving up on itself completely, told Inacio that she was an angel sent from God to bring him to Heaven.

Ivana's mind told her that Inacio was already dead, and now they had to wait until his body realized it too.

Her mind was much more reliable than his was. She did not have gonorrhea.

Before he contracted the disease, Inacio had worked for the Catano Shipping Company, which sent him all over the world. He transported soybeans, from docks to ports and back again. He was sent to Atlanta, Georgia, and spent his night with a woman he had met at a bar called "Gospel."

The woman's name was Diane Lazarus.

Before he met Diane Lazarus, Inacio harvested soybeans in Brazil. It was a dangerous job, and pests were everywhere. He was once bitten by a bat. It was a peculiar-looking creature, with bright, yellow eyes and a blunt-tipped tail, and, unbeknownst to him, it left traces of a disease in his blood. The bat died shortly afterwards, but Inacio survived after fighting off a wretched fever that had his brain racked with hallucinations. In the end, though, his immune system prevailed and left his body with the memory of how to defeat this disease. This was a trait he would end up passing along to his one and only child, a young boy, born to a woman Inacio would meet in a night club in Atlanta, Georgia.

Not that Simon Lazarus would ever know any of this. He had never met his father.

Chapter 57:
Easy Mistakes to Make

Her face wore a layer of dust and blood and her dress was torn from the shoulder. Ivana sat outside her empty church, drifting between delusions and reality, like a mosquito in the breeze. For the moment, she knew where she was, and the memories of the last few weeks returned to her, even as she wished that they would have stayed away.

She remembered getting the call that the Quarantine had fallen, but not having anyone left to report it to. She remembered seeing on the news that the President of the United States had died just after leaving Brazil. She remembered arriving at this church and seeing no priest.

It was empty and looted; the pews overturned and the tabernacle stolen. Many of the stained-glass windows were broken. Ivana could not bear to stay inside, so, in the sun and the rain, in the heat and the night, she remained outside, withering away.

She had lost her purse but she clung to her long dead cell phone. Its screen was dirty and cracked. She had been waiting for days for a call from her family. In her heart of hearts, though, when the delusions retreated momentarily and she was stable enough to admit it to herself, she knew damn well that they were all long dead.

Ivana Carvalho hadn't seen a living person in days.

Her vision began to spin on the edges, and she knew she did not have long before the delusions returned. She began to pray quietly. She began to ask the Lord for forgiveness.

Her final hallucinations came fast into her mind.

She was in the Olympic arena, sitting in her seat beside the President of Brazil, and all the thousands of eyes turned and faced her. They were vacant, and blood dripped from the gaping mouths of every face that was directed toward her. A breeze was stirring throughout the stadium.

Jorge, her friend and colleague, stood before her as if he were the Angel of Death.

"The bats, Ivana," Jorge's deafening echo accused her. "What about the bats?"

And then, their bodies all collapsed to ash before her eyes and dispersed in the breeze which rose and whipped and grew to a howling wind, loud against her ears, roaring, swirling, the ash all around her until she could not breathe but scream and then--

The wind stopped and the air cleared and she was in medical school, being introduced to a man named Pedro, with golden skin and a smile that made her feel safe. She kissed him, but his lips were cold and when she opened her eyes she was kissing his corpse as she found it after the car wreck, bloodied and broken. She screamed and then that, too, turned and began to crumble and melt away before her eyes, to be replaced by her mother, telling her she would never make a man happy if she was a doctor. Then her mother became her first medical school professor, and he was sneering at her, and she felt so, completely alone. She was being named Minister of Health. She was nine years old, and because she refused to play with the girls and their silly dolls, she was being picked last again on the soccer pitch. She was seventeen years old, and her first date put his arm around her shoulders. She was five years old, holding her young dog.

She was back in the arena, and there were only bats, bats everywhere, bats with short tails and beady, yellow eyes, flying around her in a cacophony of wings, blotting out the moon.

Suddenly, the world went silent, and through the swirling bats, in her fever dream, for the briefest of moments, Ivana thought she saw her God.

"Meu Deus?" she croaked.

Her voice was heavy, a final plea for forgiveness from a broken soul.

But it was not her God that she saw. It was only her Creator, and her sins were not mine to forgive.

They were only mine to write.

"No," I whispered.

And Ivana Carvalho was dead.

Chapter 58:
Mea Culpa

I would like to apologize for Chapter 46. Ivana was a better person than I ever realized. She did not deserve that.

Chapter 59:
Who the Hell Is Going to Read This, Anyway?

She was the only one who really read what I had to say. Best editor I ever had. Better than those bastards over at Peacock Hill, that's for sure. All they ever do is tell me how much they love everything. Hell, they'll probably even consider this paragraph genius. Hey, Jason, fuck you and your bald head. The glare blinds me every time I'm in your office.

Like he has any idea that I never sent out anything I ever wrote without her approval first.

Why did she want to go? And why can't I remember the color of her eyes?

Chapter 60:
Frosted Flakes

Simon Lazarus rose from his hospital bed and walked through the empty halls. They were mostly silent, save for a few echoing coughs and the rantings of disease-riddled minds, calling for people that were not there. The nurses and doctors had all left or passed away themselves. Simon walked through the doors into the empty city of Cleveland, Ohio.

The streets were deserted.

It had been six days since Bill Pulski had passed away and five since the last of the doctors caught the disease. Simon did not know why he had stayed in the hospital since then, and he did not know why he was leaving now, but he knew he needed to go. It was like someone was in his head, controlling his movements, directing which street to walk down, which empty apartments buildings and car wrecks to drift past aimlessly in the city that was his home.

Simon Lazarus was the last man in Cleveland.

He approached an entire section of the city he did not recognize.

That's strange, he thought.

He had lived here his entire life, after all. He ought to know the city by now. A street sign read ROTAERC ROAD. He walked down it. The buildings were packed into each other and got progressively older the farther he walked. He looked up at the windows as they reached toward the clear sky. The body of a man was hanging out of a window seven stories up. Simon wondered what his favorite breakfast cereal was.

He continued along the road. At the end of the street, there was an old-looking gray stone building. This felt like the place he had to go to. He approached the heavy wooden doors, twice his height at least, pushed one open and stepped in.

Chapter 61:
Human

"I like that bit there, the one about the Frosted Flakes."

"Why?"

"It's just so simple."

"And you like that?"

"Yeah. It just feels human to me, and I love it when something can make me feel human."

Chapter 62:
Modes of Transportation in North America

My mother passed away when she was struck by a passenger train in 1994. They did not know how to write that in the coroner's report, so they simply checked the box beside the word 'Trauma'.

I have never really been the biggest fan of trains. They are always trapped on their singular track, traveling from one predetermined destination to the next, never meandering off on their own. And when they do, it always seems to cause a great big fuss, so I try to stay away from them simply as a general rule. I guess I just have always preferred a wide-open ribbon of asphalt under the wheels of a nice automobile over the methodical clickity-clack of the tracks. More freedom that way. I hardly ever pay attention to the speed limit signs but, then again, who does?

I once found myself beside a lake at three in the morning. There was a singular boat, out far enough away that I could not see anyone moving about on deck. Not that they would be. Seldom is anyone up at that hour besides myself. I remember that night because it was a good one. She had leaned up against me as we gazed upon the ancient, twinkling lights painted on the inky-blue backdrop of infinity just for us, and I wondered if anyone ever really spent the time to look at the beauty of the stars anymore, and if her hair was always this soft, and why the night smelled of dust and moonbeams, and if I would be hit by a passenger train like my mother was, and if I did would it even matter at all, and what happens to the worlds inside your head when you die, and if those people are real with dreams and lives and loves of their own, and if God was an author and if he was what would that make me, and if the lake was deep enough to--

Then she kissed me.

I didn't wonder anything at all.

Chapter 63:
Reasons

"It's...not bad."

"You don't like it."

"No! No, I do like it, actually. Parts of it, anyway. It's very funny, maybe your funniest."

"You hate it."

"I don't hate it. It's just...missing something."

"Like what?"

"I don't know. Something to ground it in the real world. Right now, it's just a story about a disease in Brazil. It's not, you know, a bad story, but it's just a story. There's no real...purpose. No depth. Not the heart like you normally have in your work. It's just not believable, and if it's not believable, I have a hard time connecting to your characters."

"What do you think it needs?"

"Well, why is this story happening in the first place?"

"I don't understand your question."

"I think the story would be better served with a narrator."

"A narrator?"

"Don't laugh! It's a good idea. You could talk directly to the reader, explain how you see things, break the world apart a little bit, you know?"

"But I don't want to break the world! I like my little world."

"Oh, stop making fun of me. All I mean is that, with a narrator, you could get to the heart of the story. Explain what you're writing, and more importantly, why you're writing it."

"But I don't really think I have more of a reason for writing it. I just thought it was a decent story."

"Well then, I'd say that you should shelve it for now. Work on your other stories. Wait until you have a reason to keep writing, and when you do, write the best damn ending for it you can. It does deserve that much, after all. Everyone deserves a good ending."

Chapter 64:
Pater Noster

I looked up from the screen upon which this world existed with all its pain and misjudgments and sorrow to find that I was in a large, empty room alone. For the life of me I could not say how I got there. The ceiling was so high that I could not make it out and the light came in through the windows painted red along the sides seemed to spill without hurry through the haze of dust in the air. The light was thin, though. Moving closer to the windows, I began to make out the detail there in the stained glass of the echoing, ancient church.

It was breathtaking. Pieces of glass, they must have been hundreds of years old now, delicately placed, depicting the pain of forgotten saints as they suffered for their God. Each piece was made by hand. The time it must have taken. . .looking down the wall, the row of stories showed not just what was on them but also the care that went into them--the greatest work that would never be seen of a man whose name would never be remembered. This church was the oldest building for blocks. The buildings on either side had been built too close to it, and these windows had not been touched by the light in decades. I could not stop thinking about that; that these stained-glass windows would never see the light. I stood there, staring at the beautiful, invisible world.

A tear dripped from my nose. I wiped it away.

I looked around and realized that I recognized the church. I have never been to Cleveland, but still I knew it. It was old; the wooden pews worn down and the air thick with the smell of lingering incense still floating, permeating every breath. I stood and began to walk towards the front, my every footstep echoing. I had been to church every Sunday since I was a child.

No, that's not right. I had been to church every Sunday *when* I was a child, but I could not even say now how many years it had been since I went to Sunday Mass. The last time I believed the words that I mumbled to my knees, aching against the cold marble-- I must have been a young boy.

Although I believed it once, I think. I felt like I did. It was all so familiar.

It felt like her.

I was at the altar. I don't remember approaching it, but I was there. And I recognized this place as well; it was where I saw her last. She had on the black dress she wore for our ninth wedding anniversary. God, she looked so good that night. She laughed at my jokes like we had never fought and when we went to bed it was like we were kids again and when I woke up before her in the morning she looked just exactly the same way she did there on the altar. Serene. Beautiful. Asleep.

That would have been nice, but it wasn't true. The casket wasn't open, it was closed. You can't have an open casket when the body has a hole in its head. They all said it wasn't my fault, that there's no way I could have known. Those were their words anyway. What they were really saying was, How could you have not known? It's the same question I've been asking for seventeen days.

I couldn't answer it, but still I wept over the box. I had wept on the altar.

I looked up through my tears now and saw the man on the tree who had died so many years ago for his courage and for his imagination.

"Is this what you wanted? Huh, is it?"

He was patronizing me. I could tell by the way he looked at me, all dolefully like that.

"Fuck you! Do you want me to believe in you? Do you even know how much I want to? How I wake up every day hoping that this day will be the one you show yourself to me? But you never do."

It had been so long since me and the man in the tree had talked, but it wasn't my fault he left me alone like that, just like it wasn't my fault the vastness of the church swallowed my words as they left my mouth, leaving me unsure if I had ever spoken at all. The only thing I was certain of was that the voice that echoed back to me was shaking. It didn't sound like mine.

"What do you want from me! I've sinned, to be sure, but I loved my wife! I was a faithful husband! I was a good father to two beautiful daughters who loved their mom too. I wrote what I needed to write. I loved who I needed to love, but you always took and took and took until now I have nothing!"

I spat on the altar.

"Why? Where were you?"

The words echoed in my head and up the vaulting parapets to a ceiling I could not see.

"Where are you now and where the fuck were you then? Would believing in you have made this all stop? Can it make it stop now? Is that what you want, you bastard, for me to believe? If that's what you wanted, then why the hell did you make me an atheist? You know I can't believe no matter how hard I try! Show yourself, you damn coward! YOU OWE ME!"

There was no reply.

"Fine, I believe! Now make it stop, make it fucking stop! You couldn't save her! You couldn't even tell me she needed saving!"

He just stared, just like the others, just like I should have known. I should have known. A thought occurred to me just then.

"But you know what, you asshole? You see this world? Do you? This world is mine! I made it. I made all of it, a fucking prick you couldn't even give a shit about, and YOU LET ME KILL ALL OF THEM! AND YOU COULDN'T DO ANYTHING!"

Why the hell was the bastard just staring at me?

"What do you want, huh? Pater noster, pah! You are not my Father! Non tibi sunt mea Pater! A Deo non iusto, a Deo spurio! Eas en infernum! ANSWER ME!"

"Hello?"

I whipped around. Someone stood in the center of the church.

"Who are you?"

"My name is Simon."

Simon? Simon Lazarus? I thought. Then, outloud, "I thought everyone was dead."

"I thought so too. I was coming here to pray. There didn't seem like there was much else to do."

I laughed. "Pray? What, to him? He can do nothing at all for you, son."

"What makes you so sure?"

"Well, this wasn't his doing. Not in the slightest. It was mine."

Simon didn't reply. I didn't want him to, so I didn't let him. After all, he needed some time to begin to process this information. When he was ready, when I was ready, he replied.

"What do you mean this was you?"

I knew he would have a hard time believing it because I wrote him that way. I knew I would have to show him. So I grabbed his hand and we were in the streets of Paris and saw the totality and the destruction of my plague. We were in the halls of Petra, the last men to ever see the ancient stone walls carved so intricately into the Jordanian mountains. We were at the church in Brazil and saw Ivana's body lying, indistinguishable from her fellow parishioners, strewn about the parking lot. And in this way, we saw the whole of the world and we never left the church in Cleveland all in one second, and the breadth of the world stood before us and under us and within us.

I let go of his hand and he understood. I waited for him to prostrate himself, to praise me.

He hit me in my face as hard as he could.

I was so stunned, I had almost forgotten that I had written for him to do that.

Had I?

"This...is you? This is all you?"

His voice, it was quivering. From rage, most likely, or pain. Or both.

"My friend, my father who left my mom, this fuckin' misery I have been having to deal with my entire life, was all your fault?"

I rubbed my jaw. "You're not the only one with problems, you know that? I could end you now if I wanted to."

"Yeah? Well, why don't you, huh? You could have made me President! You could have made me rich. You could have made me handsome or famous or at least not killed everyone I've ever known! But you did this," --he gestured around to the empty room that no doubt had a street littered with bodies just beyond-- "instead! Why? Why did you do it?"

I didn't remember writing this part. I didn't have anything to say. He continued.

"What do you want from me, huh? What did I ever do to you to deserve this? I didn't ask for you to make all this and I certainly didn't ask to be the last one here!"

"I don't--"

"Don't what? Care? Understand? Why the hell did you even do it in the first place?"

He was close to me now and I could see the fury that brought tears to his eyes, and I could feel them in mine as well.

"I'm sorry."

I couldn't hear myself, and I'm not even sure if I spoke the words aloud. It didn't matter, he knew what I said. Of course, he knew what I said.

"I just don't," --he took a deep breath-- "understand."

"She killed herself, Simon. I loved her, and she chose to die. And I'll never know why she wanted death more than she wanted me, but part of me died with her. I didn't know what to do. I don't think I ever will. I needed something, something that was mine. I needed a release."

"And so this?"

After a second, I nodded.

"But why all the pain? Why all the destruction? You could have made something beautiful. You could have made something happy, something of love. But you made this?"

"I wanted to make art."

"You made pain!"

I looked up at the cross. The sad eyes of the man who hung there were quiet, like the church. I stared at them for a long time. When I turned back to reply to Simon Lazarus, he was gone, as if he had never been there.

Which, of course, he never had.

I paid for my tab, shut my computer, and left the bar.

245

THE END

Acknowledgments

The first draft of this book was 12 pages long and written in the Summer of 2016. In it was only Chapter 1, Chapter 62, and Chapter 64.

The only feedback I got at the time was "I like it, but you should write more."

So I did.

And much in that way, Cleveland started to grow. Over the course of six years, sometimes in large bursts and sometimes by inches, Cleveland began to be realized. All the while, I had people pushing me in the right direction. They carried me, encouraged me, and, if I'm being honest, tolerated me in my more obnoxious moments. That they still love and support me is an honor of which I will be eternally as grateful as I am baffled.

The amount of people I need to thank for how this story came to be is innumerable, but there are several who deserve to be recognized directly.

To the Curious Corvid team, who took a chance on a book about a plague in the middle of a plague. You've made this a dream come true.

Alan Brown, the first person in the industry of literature to truly believe that there was something special about Cleveland, and to whom I owe an immense debt for working unusual hours to help me develop both the story and my own skills. Our calls, held during extra-long lunch breaks, 5 AM mornings fueled by bitter coffee, and even the occasional call that would inch close to midnight have done more to develop me as a writer than anything I could have possibly hoped for.

My family, who supported me to pursue writing at a young age. Without their encouragement, I never would have been able to build a project like this.

My friends, the people who became my family long before I realized it was happening. If only there were room and time enough to thank you all individually; one day, I promise I will.

To Melanie Rose Callihan, my beautiful girlfriend, who encouraged me to keep going when I was on the brink of giving up. She was next to me when I received my offer letter from the Corvid team and was the reason I queried them in the first place. I don't know where I'd be without you, but wherever it would be, I know I'd be there missing you.

And lastly to everyone I've ever stolen from. Whether it be your name, your thoughts, your affect, or a simple sentence you didn't think I'd remember. I did. Thank you.

Writing a book is an exercise in compilation, pulling together scattered thoughts and wrestling them into a single shape, until one day, when you least suspect it, there it is. And so, most importantly, thank you, reader, who gave these thoughts your time.

I'll see you in the next book.

Danny O'Dea is from a small town just on the outskirts of the Blue Ridge Mountains, where the Earth itself is at its oldest and most humble. He studied literature and politics at the College of William & Mary before working in education and communications. His first novel, The Last Man in Cleveland, was published in the early Spring of 2022. O'Dea currently resides in Charlottesville, VA, with his lovely girlfriend and their golden retriever, Juniper.

www.ingramcontent.com/pod-product-compliance
Lightning Source LLC
Chambersburg PA
CBHW060303310726

48976CB00007B/2186